First Person Singular Vol. 3

More Very Short Stories of Wit & Wisdom

Ross Ulysses Munroe

Manor House

Library and Archives Canada
Cataloguing in Publication

Title: First person singular / Ross Ulysses Munroe.

Names: Munroe, Ross Ulysses, author.

Description: Contents: Vol. 3 More very short stories of wit & wisdom.

Identifiers: Canadiana 20190239891 | ISBN

9781988058726 (v. 3 ; softcover) | ISBN

9781988058733 (v. 3 ; hardcover)

Classification: LCC PS8641.L97 F57 2019 | DDC
C813/.6—dc23

Cover Design-layout / Interior- layout: Michael Davie
Cover art: Oneinchpunch / Shutterstock
Edited by Virginia Munroe
First Edition

144 pages / 27,284 words.
 All rights reserved.
Published November 2021
Copyright 2021
Manor House Publishing Inc.
452 Cottingham Crescent, Ancaster, ON, L9G 3V6
www.manor-house-publishing.com (905) 648-4797

Funded by the Government of Canada

For Mackenzie,
our glorious daughter.

Introduction

There is a diamond — so clear, so transparent, unsullied by earthly matters and what matters not, which can only be apprehended by that which it reflects, a mirror without form. One that is cut so precisely, its edges are capable of rending mundane experience into ribbons, yielding the fleshy fruit that resides inside, yet remains unblemished.

To look into any facet is to see unfolding phases of the moon, a kaleidoscope of change, of fabricated identifications. And the source of it all can be hunted by following the traces back to where they converge. So it is with the stories in my life, and in this book.

A Little Swearing From Readers

'What a remarkable and vivid set of books -- style sharp, economical and concise, almost hard-boiled. And what a breadth of subject matter in such slim volumes, everything from Arctic Adventure to Advertising Angst with Kafkaesque fantasiess and Zen koanlike musings in between. Can't wait to read the sequels!' *Neil Ross*

'A tour de farce!' *Susan Gerovsky*

'Beautiful writing in stories well told...' *Lisa Bostock*

'Beautifully written!' *Ann Urban*

'Great short stories! Ross is one of the best around!' *Mitch Gold*

'I love the stories - they're beautifully written!' *Fern Levitt*

'Delightful, masterful storytelling!' *Karim Mirshahi*

'AWESOME!' *Jocko Crerar*

'Beautiful work!' *Maria Ricossa*

'Very visual writing...' *Tom Fiore*

'I love this... Thanks for the journey, Ross!'
Kenneth John McGregor

Table of Contents

9

The Book of Life

Rodney Dangerfield Gets No Respect. Again.

Poor Rodney. He never got any respect at the best of times. Even when he was playing himself.

My Creative Partner, Eugene, and I were racking our brains for a radio campaign idea for Monroe Shock Absorbers. Eugene hit on the idea of using a Rodney Dangerfield sound-alike to produce a series of funny spots focusing on the comic.

Sadly, the budget was very lean at $5,000, so we couldn't afford the real guy.

Eugene started casting for the talent and I started working on the scripts. It was a piece of cake:

'The springs squeak so much in my car, I got into it last night thinking it was my mattress. I couldn't find my wife there either…' (Drum roll)

'My car does so much Rocking & Rolling, I've been thinking of joining a Heavy Metal band…' (Drum roll)

'Every time I get into my car, I get the shock of my life! So yesterday I called an electrician…' (Drum roll)

And so it went for ten executions, the client loved the idea and Eugene found the perfect wannabe Dangerfield. The recording session went flawlessly, and we spent the afternoon laughing our martinis out with the client in the boardroom afterwards.

Until he said 'Of course you got the approval of his agent…' Without missing a beat, Eugene lied: 'Of course!'

That's when we started pulling our hair out. But Eugene had the idea of calling Rodney's agent, and making him an offer he had to refuse: We record ten spots with Rodney and pay the agent the grossly minuscule amount of five thousand Canadian dollars. With a complete buyout!

He'd have to turn it down.

The next day, when Eugene called the agent, Rodney himself answered the phone. Backpedaling, Eugene protested: 'I didn't mean to disturb you, Mr. Dangerfield. I was looking for your agent…'

'You're talking to him! I fired my agent!!!'

When Eugene explained the sorry state of our finances, along with the fact that we were planning on hiring a sound-alike, Rodney asked how much we were paying the poor slob.

'$5,000 – Canadian' Eugene says.

"I'll take it!!!' Rodney bellows. 'This is why I fired my agent. He would have passed! What am I, made of money?"

Which would have been a real coup for us. If we hadn't already blown the budget. As it was, we had to tell him the client was still deciding and we'd get back to him.

Praying he never stooped to tuning in any Canadian radio stations.

The last thing we heard was 'What did I tell you??? I never get any…' His voice trailed off as he slammed down the phone.

Casting Session

A beautiful summer's day early in the morning.

A relaxing drive, sailing down the highway to Port Dover, Hendrix transforming the landscape with *All Along The Watchtower*.

I pull up to the pier and scan the length of it, a dozen fishermen sitting slumped, already half-baked and utterly demoralized.

I get out my gear as if I were Clint Eastwood and step onto the concrete, pausing. They all turn to give me the once-over. There is only one spot to claim as my own, right at the end of the Long Walk.

I begin to march toward glory, though feeling a bit overdressed in my hip waders flopping around me, with two nets slapping my backside with each step as I stride past their twisted, smirking pasty-assed faces.

I reach the end and unsling all eight feet of my brand new Fenwick rod. I look back at the onlookers and arch an eyebrow. They're jealous I am guessing, sensing that the perfect combination of equipment and expertise is about to unfold in front of their hungry eyes.

I turn and scan the water. Sometimes a glimmer of sunlight can be the first thing that is caught, its reflection apparent as the fish turns in pursuit of prey. It may be a Walleye, a Bass or perhaps one of the oversized Perch that Lake Erie is known for.

A Musky would be even more impressive - or Steelhead, very tasty either stuffed on the wall or into one's stomach.

The biggest of all, of course, is the One That Got Away. And anything is better than the One That Was Never There. But my mind was getting away from me faster than a 25-pound Salmon on 6-pound test.

My audience was becoming distracted so I had to take immediate action. I flipped the bail, leaned back, and cast as far as I possibly could. And with a heavy spoon at the end of the line, it was a good one!

The shiny implement sliced through the air, as my heart soared with it, even catching the wind, sparkling in the rays of the sun as it unerringly dove towards its unseen target.

Until my line hit a knot, at which point it stopped abruptly with such a force that it tore my new rod and reel out of my hands, flew through the air and plunged into twenty feet of water, sinking without hesitation, along with any hubris associated with it.

I didn't know if the gurgling I heard came from the event itself or some sort of myocardial infarction on my part.

When I turned and looked back down the pier at all the probing eyes before me, I took a deep breath and began the Long Walk back to the car, bereft of both my fishing tackle and my dignity.

With each step, it began to seem more like a gangplank.

Coming of Age in the WannaBe Tribe

I was a member of the WannaBe tribe.

Our bows were strong, our canoes were long and our braves were legendary, renowned as fearsome warriors.

Our war chants echoed across the lake, striking terror into the hearts of the BigWolf tribe and lesser creatures, who probably trembled at the mere mention of our coming.

Now tribal lore had it that whosoever lived by the WannaBe Code shall be rewarded by A Great Miracle.

For the uninitiated, the WannaBe Code was strict in the extreme, designed to build muscle and strengthen the heart. 'When the morning bell rings, you must join the men in the village clearing, even if you're having a dump. Don't even bother to pull up your pants', we were told!

Once we were all assembled, the chants began:

'We are WannaBe, our arrows fly

Our axes made to circumcise.

Our spears unleashed explain what's what

As they stick our enemies in the butt!

We are WannaBe!'

Then we'd round the whole thing off with that old WannaBe favorite:

'Don's belly is full of jelly!'

Don was Grand Chief of the tribe, and though he weighed as much as two pregnant buffalos, he was still wily enough to teach us the Way of the Woods.

Important skills handed down through the last year or two included How to Sharpen a Stick, I can Spit Farther than You Can and How Old am I Anyway? Safety procedures were not ignored. What to Do When You Set the Tent on

Fire While Smoking that First Cigarette; Escaping from a Swarm of Angry Wasps after You Throw Sticks at their Nest; and, finding The Giant Stone That Makes You Go Pee When you Sit On It, were all important life lessons.

The highlight of the summer was celebrating your birthday if you were lucky enough to have it fall in July or August. That's when the cake would come out — and believe me, it wasn't made of beef jerky, or pemmican for that matter. And it included Neapolitan ice cream and candles, plus several rounds of Happy Birthday to boot.

The only problem was I was born in May. I often descended into a blubbering mass of self recrimination and regret, cursing my fate in a manner unbecoming of the WannaBe brave.

One night when the moon was full and the forest was a-hoot with owls, I prayed so fervently to the Great Spirit, that I came to know that I was to be visited with my own special Great Miracle, else what are Great Spirits for?

A week later, my older brother, Bob, was tracking a bear or on some other exciting evening adventure the older kids at Camp BigWolf across the lake often had, when he heard the entire WannaBe tribe in song: 'Happy Birthday to You! Happy Birthday to You! Happy Birthday Dear Ross! Happy Birthday to You!'

He sneaked up to Camp WannaBe and sure enough, there I was chowing down on WannaBe Black Forest cake and mountains of WannaBe ice cream, with my fellow braves furiously dancing in a circle around me with glee.

Obviously the Great Spirit told somebody my birthday was, in fact, not in May, but this very hot summer's day.

I forgot about the whole thing once I turned eight. But from that day forward, my guess is that my brother must have come to believe in Great Miracles himself, given the remarkable turn of events.

Bar Shots

The Corona Bar, 82nd Avenue, Edmonton, Saturday 1:17 a.m. Badly-named these days and bad news back then, when it drew dozens of patrons in droves every night looking for far more than a few shots. And a hot date they could disappoint the next morning.

I'm with my buddy Mark. We look around. It's late and by the time the ladies begin to strut their stuff in earnest, the men are scarfing down so many shots, they're fighting already.

Their affair is really with each other.

Some dude is so riled up, he walks in the double doors with a .30-06 Springfield and starts shooting everything that moves. Except he's seeing double.

Instead of hiding under the tables, every mother's son of them surges toward the shooter like a twister in a dust bowl. And they all proceed to beat the interloper unconscious.

That takes the steam out of their whistles, and they settle down for a few more shots of their own.

Then — and only then — the cops work up the nerve to swagger into the bar. No rush, though.

It's just another Saturday night at the Corona.

One Night in Monte Carlo

I once had the great good fortune to shoot Alex Pangman singing *One Night in Monte Carlo* for Bravo TV. The connection with Alex was suggested and arranged by the inimitable producer, showman and on-air JazzFM host Jaymz Bee, and I met the two of them in a trendy Cabbagetown grotto to discuss the details.

Over a few glasses of wine, we developed a jazz video concept that intercut Alex and her swing band performing with Safari-clad marionettes, on their exotic journey 'across the Atlantic' and somewhere in the south of France atop a camel, an elephant, a flamingo and the like.

We all agreed the approach was perfect and with that, they left. I could hardly wait to call 'Action!'

Sitting alone for a moment, I realized the joint wasn't jumping and was now nearly empty; just a bartender cleaning up at back and two guys in a booth by the door.

Still feeling the afterglow of the pinot and a successful preproduction meeting, I got up and sat down with them uninvited to chat a bit before leaving.

At first, they were taken aback. Then they noticed I had a buzz on, and they began exchanging sideways glances. I could tell from their body language that they thought I was trying to pick them up, and was an easy mark to be rolled, possibly including some fisticuffs and a stabbing or two.

Realizing my predicament, I played along, but I could tell the demands and the violence were close at hand.

Suddenly, I held up my index finger and said 'Wait! I've got something for you — I'll be right back!!!'

With that, I stood up and sashayed slowly out the door. Once it closed, I ran like hell to my car and drove off.

Sailing the World

I got a book about how to build wooden boats, with a few pieces of wood and a few nails. In no time, I had a flotilla of warships: battleships, destroyers, cruisers and more in battle formation in the basement.

Building on my success, my imagination got the better of me, and I realized I could put together an actual raft, one I could sail down at Princess Point, perhaps out where the big fish were.

So I gathered the wood and laid out the planks, hammering and sawing, until I had an 8' x 6' raft. It was ready for the crowning glory — a 1" x 2" x 6' mast and a bed sheet for a sail.

As I rested from my labors, I took a break and started planning how to get it two miles down to the lake. Wheels pulled by my bicycle? An oversized dolly?

But I couldn't get it out through the basement door which, of course, was only a few feet wide…

That's when I began to wonder if all that wood would make a good tree fort.

Ross' Home Cooking

Ever miss that real Home-Cooked taste of the '50s and '60s? Fear not! Ross has gathered together a few of the most mouthwatering dishes that have somehow gotten lost somewhere between the Foreign Invasion of French pomp and Italian grandiosity. But we didn't cotton to any feigned accents fabricated to impress the neighbors back then, did we?

Shame, Julia Child! Go back where you didn't come from. You're bad, Marcella Hazan!!! Just because you lost the War is no reason to take it out on us.

Bonne soiree to the Lyonnaise Potatoes, the Magret de Canard, the Entrecôt; Arrivederci to the Antepasto, the Ribollita, the Tagliatelle, the Zuccotto.

Prepare yourselves for the unmistakably unique textures and tempting flavors of the North American 'Is There Anything In Here To Eat Anyway, Mom?' kitchen. But first, a few basics:

1.   Le Lait de Powder: Powdered milk is nothing to sneeze at, especially if you're attempting to pass it off as cocaine. Try not to stir it too vigorously or you may miss out on the exquisite little powdery lumps that are included at no extra charge.

2.   Margarine á la Yellow Spot: Hard to come by these days, this remarkable essential appears to simply be lard, when in fact it looks a little like butter when you mix in the Yellow Dye #10 and squint.

3.   Le Canistèr du Old Bacon Fat: The exciting thing about this one is trying to guess when you last had bacon. Plus endeavoring to discern whether those are bacon bits

or dead flies stuck in it adds to the Wow factor in the unlikely event that you happen to be entertaining company.

And now, to the food!

4.   Still-Frozen Fish Float: Simply take a package out of the freezer and let it thaw for the most part. Cut it into rectangular sections and put it in the oven. Meanwhile cook up a heaping helping of Minute rice and heat a 48 oz. can of skinned tomatoes. Once everything is ready to serve, plate the fish and pour on the tomatoes, juice and all, beside it - topping the whole affair with rice. Let stand for an hour and 45 minutes or so until the fish has reached a rubbery consistency, and the rice is floating around much like maggots doing the backstroke. It's important to pray before digging in on this one.

5.   Overcooked Chicken Livers In Corn Sauce: There's nothing quite like the confusingly irritating and psychologically damaging experience of eating overcooked chicken livers. One way to make up for its deficiencies is to really pour on the creamed corn, straight out of the can. Suddenly, it becomes a sauce! And there won't be a complaint in the house. In fact, there won't be anybody left in the house at all.

6.   SPORK & SPAM Medley: A close relative of Spic & Span genealogically, the Spork & Spam Medley is guaranteed to astonish even the most discerning taste buds! And no matter how the Chef has arranged the ingredients, one can never tell what is Spork and what is Spam, so it doubles as a family guessing game as well. Goes well with cold Lima beans and Sheriff Simulated Mashed potatoes. You can present this one with pride but, as always, make sure you have made allowances for beating a hasty exit out the back door.

7.	Head Cheese Royale: When it comes to versatility, Head Cheese moves straight to the head of the class! No need to bother cooking it. Actually, if your guests know it's on the menu, you likely won't even have to unwrap the package itself. But this royal dish is also remarkable, since it serves as both the main and the dessert. The pig's brain is certainly a smart choice on its own. But because it is jellied, it satisfies those subject to post-dinner cravings as well.

8.	Pot Luck Surprise: Always good in a famine, this dish can be as varied as the number of foods in your neighbor's icebox. Just pop over when the parents aren't home and say 'What's in the refrigerator?' Almost anything can happen, especially if you didn't see the Dad at work behind the appliance, and he pops up, threatening you with a large monkey wrench.

9.	Sweet'ums Sugar Balls: This is easier than it sounds. Take a spoonful of Margarine á la Yellow Spot. Look in the cupboard to see if there's any sugar left. If there is, just roll the Balls around in the sugar and eat them. You can whip them up faster than your Mom can say 'What happened to all the sugar???'

10.	"More, Please": This is one of my favorites, and always part of every meal! Plus it's a gratifying acknowledgement for Chefs who think 'shortening' refers to cutting back on the portions, which may be a good thing.

There's an awful lot to Home-Cooked North American Cuisine than can legally be printed here. For a taste of the endless array of stomach-churning options, keep your eyes glutened to this column.

And Bon Appétit!

Please Don't Tell Them I'm at Yuri's

Secreted somewhere in the tangled underbrush of the Dundas Strip is hidden a world-renowned rendezvous that is becoming famous all over Etobicoke and even as far away as Mimico.

Hearkening back to its roots in Kyivan Rus, the establishment is aptly named Yuri's.

At first glance, it reminds one of virtually any world-renowned rendezvous one might come upon, say in Paris, Monaco or Kyiv itself.

But appearances are deceiving. A closer look reveals much more than meets the bulging eyeball.

Couples both the young and the not-so young at heart, sucking passionately on each other's chicken thighs under the tables. This high-voltage action can be spiced up according to one's individual lip-smacking preferences.

Meanwhile, lovers of every known or as-yet undiscovered gender are flinging themselves with utter abandon into the Romeo and Juliette salad. Without even taking the recommended precautions.

Former confidantes, now fallen out, are turning on each other, beating them silly with Club sandwiches.

And everywhere, one hears the moans and sighs that come at no extra charge with Cranberry Cheesecake, dripping with what is hopefully a rich Swiss chocolate sauce - enough to make one drool like a non-proverbial fool.

Listen closely and one can hear couples whispering 'Yuri Burger', to which the waitress retorts 'I am not!!!'

Or the quaint cooing of elderly lovebirds singing polkas while poking perogies.

There is a dance floor where people who aren't supposed to know each other definitely do, and The Shmooze Track, a runway the length of the bar, where people bump into each other and apologize just for the thrill of it.

Check out the legendary "Scarface" booth, a little love-nook hidden discreetly away from the attention of the media and the motion-picture industry, where people become very complicated together.

All in all, given what they concoct back in the kitchen away from the prying eyes of food critics and the Health Department alike, it is obvious that people only pretend to go to Yuri's for the food and atmosphere.

They're really there to go for each other.

The brainchild of a few upwardly-mobile potato pickers, it was originally created as a hide-out from the KGB.

These fine men were the only people ever to be catapulted against their wills over the Berlin Wall from the other side, having been convicted of inciting 'uncomradelike frolicking' amongst the masses.

And ever since they broke out of jail over here, they have undertaken a commitment to continue the spread of this humanitarian philosophy locally, starting with Etobicoke. Yuri's is only the first step.

But a word of caution: when you go to Yuri's wear your dark glasses. You might meet someone you're not supposed to know.

With someone they're not supposed to be with.

Interdepartmental Memo GNWT 81-1984.

An actual Policy put in force when I was working for the Government of the Northwest Territories.

It has come to our attention that a number of Departments have included the purchase of capital items, in their annual operating budget proposals — specifically, the acquisition of personal computing devices such as laptops, desktops and the like.

This activity is a direct contravention of Department of Finance guidelines, as established by the Department of Supply Services. As is common knowledge, the Government of the Northwest Territories (GNWT) recently conducted an exhaustive review of its finance requirements in regard to such matters, and after lengthy analysis, has determined that the new mainframe system is more than necessary for the needs of all Departments.

To that end, more than one million dollars was allocated and paid to serve the accounting needs of stakeholders across the GNWT. It has since been drawn to our attention, however, that the new system is somewhat deficient. It is unable to subtract.

For that unforeseen development, we sincerely apologize. Despite this unfortunate turn of events, the Policy prohibiting the use of personal computing devices remains in effect, since we do currently have the new mainframe in service, despite its inoperability.

We can only suggest that any necessary tasks regarding Subtraction during mathematical calculations be performed manually via adding machine or writing instrument, then incorporated into your spreadsheets as positive values only.

Thank you for your compliance in helping to avoid the redundancy of technology and in providing the best value for the tax-paying public.

Survival Tips for Sleeping in the Snow

Required Equipment:

1. Kevlar backpack with reflective tape.

2. Down-filled army mummy sleeping bag with outer moisture-proof shell.

3. Waterproof snowmobile suit with hood.

4. Waterproof mitts with detachable fingers complete with hand warmers.

5. Subzero flashlight, especially for hitch-hiking at night.

6. Cell phone with extra battery.

7. Compass.

8. Beef Jerky & MARS Bars?

9. Folding axe/army shovel.

10. Hunting knife.

11. Survival tooth brush.

12. Bear spray.

Precautions:

1. Never hitch-hike on Saturday night outside of Medicine Hat. They're drunk and they'll try to run you over with their 4x4s.

2. If a blizzard strikes, build a makeshift igloo and call it a night. In the morning, check to make sure you're alive before starting out.

3. Don't eat yellow snow where the Huskies go.

4. Don't sleep on the shoulder. Truckers pull over for the night there & squash you.

5. Stay away from snowmobile trails. Sleep by barbed wire fences if available.

6. Avoid wooded areas in grizzly country, as well as large, human-shaped feces.

7. If frostbite starts to set in, rub your hands together to generate friction. Then place them under your armpits, if you have washed them properly.

8. To circulate heat from other dimensions, focus your attention intently on your diaphragm — otherwise known as the Hara. Hold a vision of a fire emanating through your torso and into your extremities. If confronted by an attacker, hurl balls of this fire from your eyes in their direction.

Roller Derby

The hill stretched out before me, crammed with rush hour traffic. Cars, buses, bone-crushing transport trucks in fierce competition, racing each other on the way to nowhere in common.

The incline was at about a 30° angle from the summit where I stood to the bottom of the Gaussian curve 500 yards away, where personal glory or absolute destruction awaited me.

These are the minor tests of little note that entreat each of us every day. Nobody will notice, it won't be in the papers, though it might be captured by the photo radar at the stoplight partway down the hill.

By the time I reached it, I would be doing well over the speed limit, and a stoplight would be the least of my troubles, whether green, yellow or red. But these challenges must be met full-on or one sinks into the morass of mediocrity especially when one toils at a desk deep in the colon of the Ministry of Waste all day.

I had carefully timed the flow of traffic: a torrent for three minutes, a yellow light for twenty seconds, followed by two minutes of cross traffic.

I locked in this sequence over seven cycles, all the while tightening the laces on my roller skates until my ankles threatened to bleed.

It was time. I took a deep breath and launched myself into the melee. My last thought was 'This is a hell of a way to get to work.' Then there was no time for anything else.

The pavement was rougher than I predicted, but on the bright side, the streetcar tracks took my mind off that.

Skipping them at irregular intervals, I gained speed precipitously, now passing vehicles on the left and right, counting the seconds down so as to catch the tail of the traffic before the light turned red.

I dodged a cyclist who appeared from the ether, and evaded a panicking squirrel, crossing in a similar emotional state to mine. Both cost me precious seconds.

I was nearing the bottom when the light unexpectedly turned red. Ahead of me, a vehicle stopped to turn right. A bus was chugging, motionless in the left lane, waiting impatiently.

As I tore past it, a three-foot gaping hole in the road became apparent, just as the cross traffic began streaming into the intersection. I had rolled the dice and they had a snake eye on every side.

An amazing thing happens when your life is in imminent danger. Time slows down to a crawl and all your attention is galvanized by the whim of circumstance, which is fickle, remorseless and brutish.

A million years of adrenaline is activated, supreme attention is paid to every frame of the 28 images per second captured by the eye, the will to live hanging on every ugly detail, without thought or pretense or a shred of self-consciousness.

Because there isn't time for anything so disingenuous and the penalty for an idle moment of distraction is death. Only the seamless fusion of body and mind offers any redemption at all.

My senses were never so sharp, nor my flesh so willing. At 10,000 feet per second, the film in my head recorded micro-changes as I tracked the moving perimeter of the pothole and hugged it, just missing the bus.The drivers proceeding crossways didn't even have time to brake as the blur formerly known as me flashed between two of them, and onto another day at the office.

When I rolled out of the elevator, I skated directly over to HR and gave my notice.

A Valentine for Aurora

Today is October 6th, the anniversary of the passing of my wife Virginia's daughter from breast cancer. So it is only fitting, among other tributes, to memorialize the role she played in our 35 mm movie, Valentine.

Had Aurora not been my step-daughter, I'd have still cast her as the lead in the movie, because of her talent, her wit, her depth of heart and her radiant good looks.

Among many other powerful moments during the shoot, one in particular comes to mind. After holding it all together up to this point, the protagonist suddenly breaks down in the boardroom of the pharmaceutical employer and descends into a fit of hysterical crying, when she realizes the emptiness of her life.

Because this scene was so critical, I had to think of a way to cause her to actually break down, rather than simply acting out the part.

When we were ready to go, with all the other eight actors around the table miming the silliness of their vocational machinations, I told the Director of Photography to get ready to shoot, but not to stop until I said 'Cut!'

Then I told him to roll film. Instead of immediately yelling 'Action!' I paced up and down the boardroom behind the actors, paying special attention to Aurora for a good 60 seconds. The tension built and built again until the table itself began to sweat.

Then, at the top of my lungs I screamed 'Action!!!'

Aurora was so startled and frightened, she immediately broke down with anguished cries, the power of her character's crumbling façade caving in on her.

Now all these years later, this story stands as a testament to her remarkable openness and sensitivity, among so many other talents… Stay little Valentine, stay…

Gun Play

I grew up loving guns. Perhaps it's because I am half American. Perhaps I should have been a die-hard PaleoConservative, but somehow those left-wing pinko socialists got hold of me.

I remember building an elastic band launcher at the age of seven, possibly given the design idea by my older brother. It was a one by two inch board with a nail in one end and a clothespin in the other.

The band was looped around the nail and stretched to be held in place by the pin.

With one squeeze, you could pick off a fly at ten paces. To improve its firepower, I assembled five pins on a single weapon, for rapid-fire fly-flattening action. And it was a bloodbath.

Despite my dad's distaste for guns, he got me a G.I. Joe Sharpshooter rifle for my birthday. But all it did was sharpshoot sparks. There had to be another way.

Soon I had saved up enough money to buy a pellet gun, even though I wasn't allowed to own one. Then I went hunting.

The only problem was there wasn't much game in downtown Hamilton. So I started shooting at sparrows. They flutter about together in bushes and I thought they'd be easy pickings.

After a half dozen tries, I actually hit one.

Aghast, I rushed over to see what I'd done. It was stone dead, a hole right through his chest where his little heart used to be. I realized right then and there I could kill one any time I pleased.

But I could never bring a single one back.

Hercules & The Bloody Battlefield

We were shooting a half hour independent drama about a spy in Ottawa, Canada, and although the Director, Dave, had put the project together at great personal cost, I was producing.

He toiled for months on the script with his creative partner and lead actor, Neil, and pulled every favor he could beg, bribe or extort from his buddies in the CBC.

He scoped out the locations, timing the shoot so the protagonist could crash through the regalia of the Changing of the Guard in front of the Parliament buildings, nearly knocking the bearskin hats off a dozen of them.

Luckily their rifles weren't loaded. After all, this was Canada.

He talked his way into Trenton Air Force Base, even seconding a military flight crew complete with army jeeps and an RCAF Hercules transport plane at no cost, having explained to the Base Commander what wonderful press their participation would confer on Canada's underwhelming military forces.

He marshaled the crew, wrangled the camera and equipment, arranged the transportation and craft services, sourced the props and arranged for post production virtually single-handedly.

I think I was brought in as Producer at the last minute simply to fill out the Above the Line credits, though I did what I could.

On the shoot day, Dave showed up thin, unshaven, exhausted and quivering with anxiety. But we went at it full-tilt boogie and got all our shots just in time to shoot the scenes at the Base.

When we arrived, the Hercules was ready for us and the lieutenants and captains dressed with all the spit and polish one could ask for.

Since time was short, we quickly positioned the crew and equipment. We had a vague feeling that reports of our activities might be working their way up through the chain of command, and we'd better wrap this show up quickly before some bureaucrat pulled the plug.

The actors were in place, and a quick rehearsal was in order. The lead was to be driven by Jeep to the plane, accompanied by three enlisted men, and leap out, running up and into it, in a mad attempt to make his getaway.

The rehearsal went off without a hitch. Until the Director keeled over on the tarmac, unconscious, and began to have a seizure. His head pounded on the concrete in rapid-fire succession, and thick, ruby-red blood began pooling out from under his skull.

Everybody was aghast, and it was only several heartbeats later that we could comprehend what happened.

"An ambulance! Somebody get an ambulance!!!" Which was already in the garage, since this was a Canadian Forces installation.

"He's an epileptic," we explained to our uniformed compadres. But we knew he'd been up all night prepping for the day and snorting cocaine. As the EMS pulled away, sirens blaring, the Captain turned to me and gave his condolences.

But they couldn't keep their assets on hold for us. I pleaded with him to get an extra two hours, and he relented.

"You know you have to direct this yourself," my associates told me. "He won't get out of the Emergency Room in time. We'll never gain access again, and everything he worked for will be for nothing."

I was on the horns of a dilemma. Between a rock and a hard place. Damned if I did and damned if I didn't. Not quite up a creek without a paddle though, I thought, and certainly not screwed six ways to Sunday.

But if I didn't direct it Dave was out of luck. And if I did, it would destroy his lifelong dream.

"Let's go get him," I said, against their advice.

We spent twenty minutes locking down the set and roared off to the hospital. When we got there, he was just coming around, his head in a bandage and his spirits sagging to the breaking point.

"He's okay," the doctor assured us. "It's just a scalp wound. The bleeding can be profuse, but no serious harm done. We'll need to keep him overnight."

Wonderful! I told him. "I just need to borrow him for 90 minutes."

Before the doctor could sputter a word, we wrestled Dave off his gurney and dragged him into the production vehicle.

We made it to the Base with 40 minutes to spare, shot the scenes and packed it in. Then we bypassed the hospital altogether, and drove directly home.

Leaving more than a little blood on the battlefield.

How I Beat Albert Einstein   at Chess

It is widely known Albert Einstein was a buddy of former world chess champion (and mathematician) Emanuel Lasker – and was no slouch at chess, though he disliked the competitive aspect. Nonetheless, he was a skilled player, even though he never really pursued the game.

My own Theory of Relativity posits that any relative of Einstein's carries the same genes and is, therefore, an adulterated iteration of the super-genius himself.

In essence, it means that often winning a number of the matches I play with my buddy Mitchell L. Gold remotely (currently continuing his studies of sacred aboriginal practices in the Yucatan) automatically confers upon me certain rights vis-à-vis his illustrious near-ancestor. Here's his point of view: *"Ross: there must be some bragging rights attached to the idea that you regularly beat a relative of Albert Einstein at chess. See below…Mitch"*

Genealogical summary: Mitchell Gold →Marguerite Sarah Gold, his mother →Rose Gutstein, her sister →Joseph Gutstein, her husband → Dvora (Dora) Gutstein, his mother →Moishe Nissan Singer, her father →Wolf Singer, his father →Maria Kohn Singer, his mother →Alexander Bondy, her brother →Ann Newmann, his daughter →Mary Lee, her daughter →Harry I Lee, her husband →Maynard Charles Lee, his son →Edith F. Lee, his wife → Hattie Schwarz, her mother →Felix (Veit) N. Einstein, her father →Hirsch Veit Einstein, his father →Veit Hirsch Einstein, his father →Ruppert Einstein, his brother →Abraham Ruppert Einstein, his son → Hermann Einstein, his son → Albert Einstein, Nobel Prize, Physics 1921, his son.

It's similar to: Asa begat Josaphat; and Josaphat begat Joram; and Joram begat Ozias; And Ozias begat Joatham; and Joatham begat Achaz; and Achaz begat Ezekias etc… only shorter and with a PhD. That's Checkmate, Al.

My Near-Fatal Science Career

I suppose I was influenced by one of my younger brothers. A Microbiologist now, he always had an interest in biology. There was the time he wanted to see if he could grow laboratory mice with webbed feet.

In an aquarium, he constructed two platforms: one with just enough room for the food and one with enough room to sleep. So they'd have to swim day after day, and through generations and the wonders of evolution, adapt.

Somehow, some lab mice got loose, and were breeding all over the house. I got an idea. I wanted to find out if a mouse would have the courage to face mortal danger in order to survive. When everybody was out of the house, I captured one and took him down into the basement.

I rigged some old Varsol rags into a circle about five feet in diameter and placed the mouse in the middle. According to my calculations he would not cross the line because of the fumes, yet he wouldn't be burned if he stayed put. But if he had the moxy to get free, he'd be through the fire line before it could affect him, which I estimated would be approximately 6" high. So I began my observations by igniting the combustible material.

The entire house almost blew up.

Not only did flames immediately shoot six feet into the air, threatening to set the ceiling ablaze. But there were dozens of half-opened cans of paint thinner, oil-based paints and more just feet away about to explode in a rain of fire. The air was dense with noxious gases, as I began desperately smothering the flames with clothes from the laundry room, coughing and gagging the entire time.

Finally it was out. If the mouse was smart he'd have made a quick getaway. I didn't find the body, so he must have made a run for it. Thank heaven I had no interest in nuclear physics.

Thin Ice

It started out well enough, but it might have augured what was to come, foreshadowing what throwing caution to the winds might portend.

It was spring breakup and Jocko and I were down at Cootes Paradise, looking across the bay to the other side, a mile or so away. The cracks in the ice beckoned to us, and we began jumping over them, one by one.

In our exuberance, we didn't notice that the ice sheet was turning into ice floes, large at first, then successively becoming smaller. By the time we realized it, we were a third of the way to the other side, and to retreat would be a sign of defeat. So on we went.

The floes had shrunk to about three feet across and they were sinking under our weight. As they sank, the water flooded over, soaking us to the bone.

Only two feet wide now, they dropped below the waterline as we each landed, hitting the water with every plunge, then scrambling up to lunge at the next. By this time we were freezing, tired and out of breath.

But it was too late to go back. At a point like this, you either give up or time dissolves and your mind becomes consumed by the will to live. Somehow, we made it to more solid footing, only to be confronted by an ice-free channel a good thirty feet wide.

Nature enthusiasts gawked as they strolled by, while we dove into the bay and swam to shore as if our lives depended on it. And indeed they did.

The Police News

Having been a Globe and Mail paperboy for years, and read it cover to cover for almost as long, I was drawn to the printed word. So when I looked in the classified ads for a job at the age of seventeen, I was excited to find one at The Police News.

'You have to start in Sales and work your way up,' they told me. 'But you get to start right away — on Commission too!!! Then they led me to a grubby cubicle in the Telemarketing Department, and handed me a script and the Yellow Pages.

The script began something like:

"Good morning Sir/Madame. I'm calling from The Police News and we're asking for your support. We are doing a lot of good work in the community, and we know as a business owner, you appreciate all the services the Police provide. That's why we hope you'll run a business-card sized ad in our publication…"

Well, I had been really good at selling newspapers in my career thus far, so I gave it a whirl.

Three hours later, I hadn't made one sale. So I got a copy of the paper and opened it up. Inside were twelve pages of ads, without a single story about police affairs or anything else.

That's when I decided to look for another career. Like working as a dishwasher. I got really soaked in that one.

My Trip to The World's Fair

As usual, our parents were taking hours to pack the great, old steamer trunk, a relic of a bygone era when you'd go to Montreal from Toronto by steamship, one assumes.

But finally that old trunk was jammed full of two weeks' worth of clothing for six family members. Then it was heaved up on the roof of our new Ford, and tied down securely for the trip to the World Expo in gay, old Montreal.

The summer vacation was a normal one at first. Lots of squabbling in the back seat, my Dad taking wrong turns, my mother complaining about it. Every once in a while, she would lose her cool and turn around.

She couldn't really say 'Don't make me come back there!' with any effect, since we were speeding along the roadway to make up for lost time. So she resorted to pinching the insides of our thighs, which could be quite painful.

At times such as these, I used to take particular glee in looking her straight in the eye with no facial expression, as if I were watching TV.

And so it went for hundreds of miles until we crossed the Quebec border and joined the last, mad dash to the fair city.

But now, dear Reader, we interrupt this narrative to go airborne back in 1967, where veteran Eye in the Sky

Reporter Len Rowcliffe is in the Radio CJAD 800 chopper with the traffic report.

'Thanks for the memories, Ross!

'Well, traffic is brisk along the MacDonald-Cartier Freeway, with families coming from as far away as

British Columbia and parts North — all filled with the promise of the celebrated World Exposition in Montreal, the City of Saints!

'The vehicles are moving along at a good clip, accident-free for once and — but wait! There seems to be some kind of snarl here. We're going in for a closer look.

'Yes, I can see it now. One of the cars has a large steamer trunk on the roof and it has opened — clothes flying out and onto the highway in a constant stream…skirts, T-shirts, pants, each one sailing through the air at sixty miles an hour and onto the Freeway!

'The cars behind it are swerving to avoid them — it's amazing there hasn't been an accident…

…the vehicle seems to be pulling over onto the shoulder now…one of the doors is opening and A YOUNG BOY HAS JUMPED OUT OF THE CAR AND IS RUNNING BACK ONTO THE HIGHWAY INTO ONCOMING TRAFFIC.

'Oh my heavens, he was almost hit that time!

'He's avoiding the cars for the moment and picking up underwear, socks, shoes, you name it…and — he's still at it now, showing some skill as he weaves and dodges in the face of what should be certain death, cars everywhere!

'Now if this isn't an unbelievable opening to the World's Fair…and it'll go down in the record books! Who in the world would drive down the road at highway speeds without locking the luggage in???'

At this moment, our extended family was listening to the radio, waiting for us to arrive from Toronto and make a grand entrance.

My grandfather looked at my uncle in disbelief.

'It isn't…it wouldn't…it couldn't really be them…could it?' he said.

Fired

To paraphrase Hunter S. Thompson, the advertising business is a cruel and shallow money trench, a long plastic hallway where thieves and pimps run free, and good men die like dogs. There's also a negative side.

An Account Director I worked closely with was once hired at a hefty salary at another ad agency with only one job to do: to get his client, the company's Marketing Director, fired.

This Marketing Director had been quietly making arrangements to switch the advertising account to another agency, where he had a buddy. The solution was to get him fired and replaced by someone in the company who would keep the account with its existing agency.

After three months of well planned set-ups, hidden traps and meticulous documentation by the agency Account Director, that's exactly what happened.

Of course my Account Director friend at that agency didn't last much longer at his new job, himself.

Since he had manipulated the Marketing Director into getting let go, my associate knew where the body was 'buried'. He had become the smoking gun.

So obviously, he had to be fired.

Road Trip to Nowhere: Day 2

You can make a lot of money in a lumber camp, and the food is great. That's what I heard and why would they lie?

Before the sun even comes up, you can eat bacon and eggs and coffee and sausages and toast and pancakes and coffee and French toast and hash browns and coffee and T-bone steak and roast beef and more.

Then you can go back for seconds. But don't worry, you won't gain any weight. And if you're still hungry, lunch is just around the corner.

So Mark and I cobbled together a couple of fellow wayfarers and set off on a road trip to Super Natural British Columbia to make our fortunes and have breakfast, in his dusty old '66 Chevy.

Once the prairies start, you can basically tie down the steering wheel and point it at the coast and you wouldn't' miss it by much.

You might catch a fleeting glimpse of the Provincial Bird - Pedioecetes Phasianellus – but they all seem to have flown the coop, like everybody else.

Or you could while away a few hours wondering why the motto is Multis e gentibus vircs!, given that there aren't any people for miles around there, but you'd pretty much be on your own with that one.

Luckily evening was falling, and there was even less to see. So without much more to do - we were tired of the word games and the 8-tracks – we decided to manufacture a wake-me-up. We had dozens of 24" fireworks sparklers in the trunk to announce our west coast arrival, and affixed a stack of them to the Chevy at all points of the compass, lighting them ablaze.

Then we jumped into the car and hit the gas, speeding down the TransCanada Highway at top speed like a flying birthday cake making a prison break, having delivered its illegal file to the lucky inmates.

It truly was a thing of beauty and cars on both sides pulled over and screeched to a halt, out of respect and a wondrous awe at what was possible if you were willing to push the itinerant envelope to the point of bursting on the scene. We had to stop intermittently to rearm. If we'd only remembered the confetti and the streamers. Just as well though, because before the turnoff to Estevan, Saskatchewan, we heard the wind wailing in the distance over the plains that sounded vaguely familiar.

It could have been the cries of the Valkeries summoned back to life by our sacred, highway bonfire on wheels. It could have been the echoes of our brave ancestors as they wended their way westward once upon a while.

But it was a motorcycle cop.

We slowed down and gave him lots of room to pass, but for some reason he seemed to be focused on us. We pulled onto the shoulder and rolled down the window, as he strutted over, holding his floppy notepad like a Colt 45.

Unfortunately, we had spilled a quart of milk a thousand miles previously.

And between that noxious assault on the olfactory senses – one which we were all no longer susceptible to – and the chemical gases issuing from molecular collisions of extra-sharp cheddar cheese, Genoa salami, cigarettes, pot and more, it was definitely worth crying over.

He made the mistake of leaning his face into the window – and yanked it out so fast, his sunglasses fell off.

'If you're looking for Alberta, it's that way,' he was kind enough to croak, pointing in all directions at once. 'Thank you for visiting Saskatchewan!' We thought he was going to escort us, but he roared away so fast, he must have had other pressing matters to attend to. Like going to Dunkin' Donuts.

Kool Skool Syllabus

After I left high school, I heard about an alternative post-secondary program out on a horse farm that seemed quite elucidating, so I tried it. Here are the details as I understood them to be:

Mission: To promote the expansion of hearts and minds through highly-unstructured, democratic learning and trial by error.

Location: Fairytale Farms.

Hours: As the Spirit dictates.

Faculty: Untenured, malcontented Marxist-Leninist Professors on their day off.

Sadly, for some reason, it only ran for about six weeks. It started off well enough, with lively discussions about astrophysics, American literature, sociology, tectonic plates & polar shifts and the like. Then after the classes, we all did a little horseback riding.

The second week, we all voted to dispense with one of the courses in favor of equine pursuits as we learned about the finer points of equestrian mastery. The third week, we voted ourselves an afternoon off. Those who wished to stay for some horseback riding were welcome to do so.

The fourth week, we did away with the astrophysics and American literature courses, and all galloped off together. The fifth week, the students didn't come to class at all, but the professors were seen out riding. The sixth week, there was no activity whatsoever at Kool Skool, other than for those who forgot it was the sixth week because they were blowing too much dope.

By that point, there was more Kool than Skool in Kool Skool.

Having a Guest for Thanksgiving Dinner

My mother was always a bit of a social activist.

When the chicken was off a tad, she had no qualms about taking it back to the store manager and 'throwing it in his face'. She refused to buy South African fruit until they ended apartheid.

She pretended to be the wife of Cabinet Minister John Munro to get a stoplight installed at the bottom of the street, post haste.

And the crowning glory to hear her tell it was to be the only person in the city of Hamilton to actually get a written letter of apology from The Phone Company for some injustice or other.

Then there was Thanksgiving. Our house was always open to wayward guests we knew who had nowhere else to go. Out would come the steaming mashed potatoes, the seasoned squash, the slivered almonds with green beans, the gravy and stuffing, and finally, the turkey itself, in all its majesty.

And of course, the Biafran.

Roughly 3.5 million Biafrans were killed in a genocide led by the British and the Nigerian government when they seceded from Nigeria. Starvation and disease were among the weapons of war.

Mother would post a large photo of such a child looking down on us from the dining room wall, before we could so much as take a bite - his wide, sub-Saharan eyes imploring silently, begging for a morsel.

I glanced at the photo, then the turkey. The poor child had less meat on his bones than the bird did. And it gave a whole new meaning to having a guest for Thanksgiving dinner. After a rousing lecture, we were ready to eat. But by this time I had lost my appetite.

Life — The Syndrome

<u>For General Release</u>

Current research has identified a condition known as Life — The Syndrome, that may affect the proper day to day predictability of certain at-risk members of the general public, such as males and females.

Symptoms can include palpitations of the heart, heavy breathing, anxiety, unexplained excitement, elevated irritation, profuse sweating, erotic fantasies, impulsiveness, fickleness and other abnormalities.

If you experience any of these symptoms, see your Doctor and tell him or her you may have contracted Life — The Syndrome, or have been in close contact with someone who has.

Medications may provide an effective treatment.

The Ross Family of Digby, Nova Scotia

Ross Ulysses Munroe was given the name Ross in honor of his maternal grandmother's family who lived in Digby, Nova Scotia.

His grandmother's birth name was Bertha Lillian Ross but she was known as Lillian. Lillian came from a huge family, which was not uncommon in those days. There were sixteen children in her family and she was the seventh child born to Alexander Hamilton Ross and Eulalie Catherine O'Connor.

All of the children of Alexander Ross and Eulalie O'Connor are listed below in chronological order:

1. Percy Vincent born September 2, 1883 - married Caroline O'Connor

2. Cora Blanche born November 30, 1884 - married Fred O'Flaherty

3. Harry Chester born April 23, 1886 - married Margaret Grace Murphy

4. Adelaide May (Aunt May) born October 19, 1887 - married James Tidd

5. Frank Ernest born October 6, 1888 - married Birdie Sweeney

6. John Ensleigh born January 10, 1890 - married Martha Brown

7. Bertha Lillian born October 4, 1892 - married James Johnson who perished in World War I; married Roland Montague Squire circa 1924

8. Joseph Wiley born April 4, 1894 - married Ada Frost

9. France Veronica born October 25, 1895 - married Dr. Martin (Boston)

10. Kathleen (Aunt Hazel) Alberta born December 13, 1897 - married Garfield Van Tassel

11. Helen Beatrice (Sister Mary Ruth) born April 10, 1899 - died 1968

12. Eileen Gertrude (Aunt Trudy) born March 31, 1902 - married Emile (Port) Portelance - died October 29, 1993

13. Edward Leo (Father Ebby) born May 10, 1903 - died November 11, 1989

14. Evelyn Emma (mother of Roma) born June 8, 1904 - married Charles Van Tassel; married Lester Wilhoff - died April 18, 1974

15. Alexander Leroy born January 22, 1907 - married Ethel Clark Campbell

16. Gordon Stan born February 2, 1909 - died July 28, 1924

Cliffhanger

Three hundred feet high, the escarpment was full of adventures, the more attractive when a list of chores had piled up at home.

Its crowning glory was a layer of sedimentary rock, riddled with caves, and one in particular held a special magic. Tall enough to stand in, it featured a charred firepit, mysterious empty crushed cans strewn here and there, half-smoked cigarettes — some with lipstick on them! — and damp, well-worn porn magazines!!!

We'd spend hours in there, trying to figure out what was what.

But the cliff above us was calling. It was about thirty feet high. I began the climb tentatively at first, clutching the rock protruding from the edifice.

But my friend was watching and I had bragged I could do it. If I backed out, he would make sure I'd become a laughing stock around the neighborhood.

The higher I got, the more his amazement rose, until I reached the top of the façade. Just another three feet and I would clamber over the crest and into the annals of 12-year-old herohood.

But the rock I grasped popped out and I began to fall backward. Everything wound down to extreme slow motion as I lunged for another. It crumbled in my fingers. I snatched at a forlorn-looking bramble, my savior now. But the roots ripped out.

Back I flipped and it wasn't very elegant: the world spinning towards me until I hit the rocky ground full force. I lay motionless, possibly for a lot longer than was really called for.

'Ross…Ross!' my friend yelled. I was very obviously dead.

He jumped up and ran back home to spread the terrible news. Ross had climbed the escarpment and fallen off — and now he was probably dead!

For my part, after shaking off my confusion, I saw that my hands were cut and bleeding. That's when a plan formed in my head.

Thinking quickly, I rubbed blood all over my face and arms.

When I staggered down the street on the way home, other kids were whispering in awe. I wobbled into the house where my mother was cooking dinner, and collapsed in a heap on the floor.

After the shrieking stopped, everything went according to plan. I was exempt from mowing the lawn and taking out the garbage for a week, while I convalesced.

And my stature with kids in the neighborhood was assured.

Film Review

The Review:

An uncanny, incisive exploration of the angst that is the unborn child of the zeitgeist so prevalent in the postmodernist world whereby peace is a relative term that exists not as a definable absolute but as a phantasm flitting fitfully against the backdrop of the darker canvas of our base natures, issuing like a black swan event flying up from the collective unconscious and spitting Type AB blood across the atlas of our souls, spilling the contents of the cradles of civilization which then are disgorged into heinous conflict, unleashing the dogs of war.

The Reality:

A Production Assistant/film student got his effects by inadvertently tripping over his tripod while getting the camera booted up. Not realizing it was still recording, he knocked over his key light, temporarily blinding the talent, who fell backwards and got her hair plastered with gaffer tape. The shoot day was cancelled, but the edit proceeded anyway.

Chop Chop

This is my confession. Perhaps Nature will forgive me for my crime in the woods.

One of us had a hatchet from a family camping trip and it opened up a whole new world. We didn't know what we were going to do with it, but it was clearly made for chopping something.

So we hid it in a satchel and made our way up the rugged slope of the escarpment.

The going was tough, but after five minutes or so of hard slogging, we happened on a clearing with a stand of about three dozen birch trees — straight, tall and proud.

Definitely enough for a few teepees with a couple of travois thrown in, should a future adventure further afield require them.

Now, I wouldn't do it today, but at the brave age of twelve, we had no choice. So we chopped and we chipped and we hewed and we hacked.

Down they came, once towering and pristine, arcing through the air until they had all hit the ground ready for harvesting and we had too.

Only to see a nicely-mown lawn behind them, rolling down the hill towards a lovely new house. The birch trees were part of the property.

The occupants were obviously away for the day, and we didn't want to be there when they got back. Hopefully, they'd think it was the work of a marauding tribe of three-foot beavers.

So we bounded away into the woods like a couple of deer, in search of another adventure, once we had made our getaway.

There were frogs in the creek to catch and salamanders whose tails would fall off when you picked them up and hornet's nests to do battle with.

It didn't take long to forget about the birch trees. I would have said a mea culpa and a dozen Hail Marys, but I wasn't raised a Catholic.

So this is my confession, instead. Perhaps Nature will forgive me. Because I'm certain the homeowners wouldn't.

Sadie Hawkins Day

It was very 'hush, hush', so of course I secretly told everybody who would listen all about it. After flirting with Sharon Silberman for weeks, I knew she was going to ask me to the Sadie Hawkins Day dance.

As the day approached, my anticipation ballooned, hormones raging as I looked in the mirror and searched for cool ways to say 'okay'. But as the event grew closer, I began to get the feeling something was wrong.

She hadn't said a word about it. Maybe it was because I wasn't Jewish, I thought. What if my name had been Munroe*blatt*?

That's when I got a tap on the shoulder, and turned around to see Gwen Goodly, the very homely and socially-inappropriate girl in the desk behind me.

'Do you want to go to the Sadie Hawkins dance with me?' she asked. 'Yes!!!' I blurted out, before I could stop myself. I had been practicing so much, it was second nature.

Suffice it to say, we didn't live together happily ever after. In fact, I had to switch desks with somebody across the room.

Riding the Rails

When you're hitchhiking across the country, sometimes your thumb can get plumb worn out. That's when it's time to consider riding the rails.

The fond memories are with me still: the chance to take in the scenery without wondering if you'll have to pull a knife on some pervert; the hearty smell of cooking over a sterno can at fifty miles an hour; bunking down for the night and waking up in another province.

But there's always the challenge of missing your train.

I was running along the tracks, closing in on the freight train as it picked up speed. My timing had to be impeccable. Any tripping, slipping or sliding would turn me into pemmican.

Suddenly I noticed an oncoming train racing toward me, and the calculus of an impending squashing beginning to concern me.

You have to watch out for the railway ties protruding from the gravel. Getting your boot stuck in a track switch can also be an issue, especially when your attention lies elsewhere. Like on living or dying.

As my train was approaching speeds that were almost out of reach, I threw my pack up and grabbed a door handle, swinging up and into the car moments before the other train flew by.

After a bit of a breather, I got out the pemmican and started chowing down. When you're riding the rails, it's either eat or get eaten.

Office Gossip Karma

Gossip is a double-edged sword. But sometimes it's called for.

I worked at the Ministry of Natural Resources and was dating a woman in another department. She told me a coworker of hers was spreading a rumor that my married boss was sleeping with a coworker of mine.

I knew it was untrue and malicious, so I told a coworker. Who told my boss. Who confronted me. Whereupon I explained I'd told my coworker about the gossip because I knew they were friends and he should know.

Whereupon my boss marched down and confronted my girlfriend's coworker in front of her entire department, calling her out. Who then blasted my girlfriend for telling me. Who then blasted me for telling the injured party.

Are you with me so far?

So two years later in an advertising agency, I heard my secretary gossiping about my (now) former girlfriend that the secretary's husband told her that my former girlfriend's new boyfriend had bragged that he was only sleeping with her to get work from her.

So I told a mutual friend to tell her that her current boyfriend was making a fool of her. So she broke up with him immediately, without saying how she knew.

So he got mad at my secretary's husband and pulled some work from him. So he got mad at his wife. Then I heard my secretary on the phone bemoaning the fact that she'd caused such a ruckus and cost her husband a lot of work.

Oblivious to the fact that I could hear her (again) after I was the one who let the cat out of the bag the first time.

I guess what goes around comes around…

Bedroom Bust

I'd just bought 100 hits of purple microdot and was counting them in my bedroom, with my younger brother John looking on. That's when I heard my father starting to come up the stairs.

And I knocked over the pill jar, microdots bouncing all over the floor.

An abject terror took hold of me as I cast about racking my brains for a plan of action. By now he was on the seventh step, with just seven left to go.

In a flurry, I grabbed a blanket and spread it on the floor. I picked up some playing cards and dealt, motioning John to sit on the floor opposite me. At the moment we picked up our hands, the door popped open to reveal my father's sons hard at play.

With a blissful smile, he left us alone. It must have been a comforting thought that he knew where we were.

The Big Bust

I don't know where I got it or why, but one day I brought a breast pump to school. Like any normal teenager, I showed it around, then put it in my locker. Right beside the ounce of Acapulco Gold I had stashed there.

I promptly forgot about it, until Miss Hendry, my history teacher, asked me why I was always up to some hijinks or other. Now Miss Hendry was renowned for her storied, ample breasts, and a classmate must have been thinking of the breast pump when he blurted out 'You should see what he's got in his locker!'

'I think I will, right after class' Ms. H. replied.

All I could think about was the pot. So when class was dismissed, I raced through the halls and up two flights just in time to bust myself before she did.

And to appear to be properly embarrassed when the lady arrived for the examination, herself.

Busted

We were pretty hot. Dealing dimes of pot in Westdale Plaza out of the back of my buddy's dad's late-model Cadillac at a 300% profit, like rock stars.

Unfortunately, we had so many customers, we were spotted by an off-duty cop. And because I had just turned 16, I was charged as an adult.

In the station, the RCMP separated us for interrogation, made us empty our pockets, and I was grilled about the extent of our operation. Except that we didn't have one.

The problem was exacerbated by the fact that they had confiscated my cigarettes. With a dozen tabs of purple microdot LSD squirreled away in the pack.

'You seem like a nice young kid,' the investigating officer mused. 'How did you get mixed up in this business?'

"Just unlucky —' I said. 'The wrong friends, I guess.'

After more chatting about what a nice neighborhood I lived in and what my father did for a living, things were going so well, I thought I'd make a bad situation better by taking a gamble.

'I'm a bit nervous…could I have my cigarettes back?' He thought about it a moment then handed them over. I had to have one for appearances sake, so I got one out.

Only to see a tab of acid tumble out and roll across the floor under his chair.

That would have put the last nail in my coffin. So I lit up and put the pack in my pocket. The cop was doing so much pontificating, he didn't notice.

And I got off with simple possession and a $200 fine.

In fact, I was probably one of the only people to deal any purple microdot right in the headquarters of the Royal Canadian Mounted Police.

Road Trip to Nowhere: Day 5

I guess it was supposed to be pretty. But when one of the girls tarted up my toenails in fluorescent blue I didn't even notice.

We had been driving through the mountains for days, their majestic peaks taunting the eye with a radiant glory so profoundly relentless, it became irritating, much as they would have for our misguided forebears, years before.

Then we all crashed in a motel just outside of Vancouver. After a night celebrating our arrival, I passed out.

In the morning, we parted company and I got on a bus going to Port Hardy to make my misfortune on the railroad, servicing a lumber camp.

I forgot about the toenail bit until the whole crew was directed to the showers, presumably for delousing louts, scouring crabs and waterboarding the flea-bitten. I was still half asleep, when I saw an unruly assortment of tattoos and toothless grins staring at my painted nails and my long hair.I hadn't realized it, but this was the last refuge of escaped convicts and criminals on the lam this side of Dawson Creek. They didn't actually rub their hands together with glee, but it was only a quick introduction so I was careful not to drop the soap.

Then to the putt-putt, rolling along the track, bringing muscular biceps and muscle between the ears to the work. The rails were laid, a dozen men prying the metal into place, which became a continuous slithering snake prowling the valleys, section by section. If one was dropped on the foot, bones could be crushed.

That's when the pounding started. Five pounds of steel flying through the air over and over like an oversized jackhammer. The mental games began, to while away the rest of the eternity that made up the day under the blistering sun.

Can I sink a spike in a railroad tie in three sledgehammer swings instead of five? That's a victory. Whose face shall I superimpose on the head as the metal slams it into the wood? That's even better when placed well.

There was the big Swede whose name I seem to remember as Sven 'The Big Swede' Smorgasbord. He could hoist two railroad ties, one on each shoulder, and carry them for a half-mile.

Rick, the foreman was so surprised he told Sven to relax and take five. The Swede was outraged. Two — yes! Three — maybe. But even Sven couldn't take five.

A wolf trotted by, long and lanky, going about the business of life and death with no particular concern for the outcome.

That's when we would have had lunch, if there'd been any. But ravens are crafty. They'd pick up our metal lunch buckets and drop them from forty feet, cracking them wide open, for easy pickings. They used to watch us to find out where the daily hiding place was, then swoop in when we were too far to retrieve them before the deed was done. Laughing the whole time.

So instead we would sit on the tracks dejected and count the crosses on the mountain where Chinese immigrant-workers had plummeted into the gorge to their deaths while setting dynamite charges. They had been hoping to bring their families over.

On our day off, I practiced my guitar, while the rest of the crew was in the ATCO trailer drinking Old Crow Kentucky Bourbon straight out of the bottle. Which became plural as the day wore on.

They were boisterous. Then riotous. Then a fistfight ensued. One of the crew had nose-picker boots and kicked the eye out of the foreman for criticizing his track building technique.

Out there, that was just an eye for an eye.

The Book of Fancies

Baggage Train from Hades

It came to me in a dream, or so it purported to be. But it could have been the remnants of a past life. Or a vision of the eternal Fields of Elysium.

My Century was snaking along the river behind me, our column of Legionnaires hidden by a line of trees.

The trap had been set.

Three legions – a total of 20,000 crack troops – were stationed behind the crest of a hill in the Teutoburg Forest about a mile upstream from us, with a few dozen slaves serving as bait for the German hordes that infested the woods, supposedly waiting with the baggage train.

Once the barbarians attacked, the Legions would spring upon them and cement Germania into the collection of baubles that Augustus had taken to add to his glory.

As seasoned veterans, we were charged with preventing a German breakout as they fled. The word was, the way to vanquish these subhuman brutes, despite their towering height, was to stab up their exposed throats.

This was a place of honor. Our armor glittered in the sunlight in agreement.

Such cavalry as we had strode proudly forward towards the clamor as the battle ensued in the distance, and we quickened our pace.

The appointed hour had arrived.

The cries of wounded animals, the screams of warriors and slaves. We stopped and I ordered my men to form up, to block any attempt at escape.

But when a black butterfly fluttered by, we had an inkling what our fate was to be.

Looking each other darkly in the eye, we gritted our teeth and made our swords ready.

A discordant cacophonous din began to issue through the river valley. Suddenly across the water came our baggage train rolling wildly past, manned by hundreds of our comrades-in-arms, the wheels clattering, the wood groaning, the oxen rushing down river ahead of the melee.

We breathed a sigh of relief and cheered our fellows on. Until they came closer.

Every man of them was dead and on his way to the River Styx, beckoning us thither. As the swarm of our enemies approached, we advanced grimly, knowing we would soon be joining them.

When the fog lifted after a few minutes I heard the anguished cry of the Emperor himself echoing across the millennia: 'Germania – give me back my Legions!!!'

The Great Goose Falls Fire

It was the height of fire season in Goose Falls and the forest was a tinderbox just waiting to explode.

The Town had already gone through a harrowing grass fire on Sally Holler's front lawn that pretty well torched her pansies. Then there was that 45 Gallon drum Jim Withers burned some trash in that almost got out of control.

And the propane Bar-B-Qs all over the place were always threatening to blow the whiskers off a donkey, if they weren't lit just right. We didn't really say 'whiskers' when we told it, though; they were more like billiard balls.

But things had to be 'sanitized' before they hit the pages of the Goose Falls Village Voice. And quite a story it became — bigger than when Council voted to launch an investigation into why there were no geese within miles of Goose Falls. Or any falls, for that matter.

People started talking. On the General Store, somebody painted 'We need a fire truck — Carstan's got one and they're even smaller than we are!!! ' Once the Ladies Auxiliary started parading up and down Crude Oil Street for the cause, there was no stopping it.

Since there were no fire hydrants in Goose Falls, it would have to be a self-pumping model. And since there was no money to pay for the vehicle, it would have to be a used one. That's when the haggling started.

After all, who was going to spring for it? The Council had a real scrum about it, but the Mayor, Billy Bob Bagger, came up with the idea of holding a raffle. The winner got the truck, which he then could lease back to the Town at favorable rates, of course.

The Mayor had the tying vote, and 'Hell-Yes!!!' carried the day. Coincidentally, he subsequently also won the raffle itself, after rigorously scrutinizing the results in person.

He was simultaneously voted the Volunteer Fire Chief, in addition to his existing duties as Goose Falls Police Chief, Best Life Insurance Agent, Lodge Leader of the Benevolent & Protective Order of Elks, Grand Knight of the Knights of Columbus, Area Rotary Club President, Worshipful Freemason — and Head Elector, of all things.

On that last point, some citizens suggested it could help explain why he won all the other elections in Town, despite the many recounts.

The specifications were drawn up and the purchase was put out to tender, in line with National Fire Protection Agency (NFPA) guidelines, which state that an Approved Pumper is "[a] fire apparatus with a permanently mounted fire pump of at least 750 gpm (3000 L/min) capacity, water tank, and hose body whose primary purpose is to combat structural and associated fires."

There was real celebration when the Pumper arrived, with its shiny newly-painted 30-year-old exterior and tried & true mechanical workings. Proudly emblazoned on the side was the insignia Pumper No 5.

After a straw poll overseen by the Mayor, it was decided to roll it into the seed warehouse for safekeeping, which was dubbed the Honorary Temporary Firehouse.

The townsfolk were so overcome with joy, they started a hoedown right then and there, where considerable amounts of libation and snack foods were consumed, possibly to excess. So much so, that pretty near everybody went home and passed out. Even Elmer's Goose Falls Jug Band Finger-Pickers stopped their whining.

But about an hour later, the Town megaphone started up. "The firehouse is burning! The firehouse is burning!!!" It was the Mayor in his capacity as Chief of Police.

Luckily, he had been the first to discover a lit cigarette in the Firehouse. "Quick, we need to use the Pumper!!!" he yelled.

Like a well-oiled machine, they went to work, seven of Goose Falls' finest volunteer firefighters stumbling out of the sack and wobbling down to the firehouse. Only when they got there did they wake up enough to realize that Pumper No 5 was no more than a burned-out shadow of its former self.

And all because some idiot threw a cigarette into the piles of seed bags during the impromptu celebration. Which turned out not to be seed at all, but highly flammable fertilizer.

"Now, I wonder what damn fool did that!" Billy said, as he lit up another smoke.

By the time the news reached the papers in the city over two hundred miles away, the blaze had scorched the entire Town to a charred, smoldering wreck of a carcass hardly suitable for man or beast — even though it had already been rapidly extinguished by the Fire Chief and his brave volunteers, using only Sally Holler's garden hose.

It appeared to newspaper readers everywhere and thereabouts that our little Town of Goose Falls was cooked. And the townsfolk didn't take it very well either, despite the obvious misapprehension of the facts.

But there's always a silver lining in cases like this, and it sure lined the pockets of Billy Bob Bagger. Because he was also the only insurance agent in town. And he owned Pumper No 5.

Except for the Mayor, of course. With his new-found wealth, he was about ready to run for higher office.

Driverless

As Joni Mitchell would have it 'they used to laugh at me when I refused to ride on all those double-decker buses because there was no driver on the top!'

But what if there were no driver on the bottom either?

Now I'm no Luddite. I appreciate having The Clapper to turn the lights on and off. I can't function without my programmable coffeemaker. I can put up with GPS technology that talks back to me, even out of turn, and voice activated word processing and radio commands are second nature.

I didn't even think too much when my new car drove over to my house after the online purchase, delivering itself. But once there, the driverless function suspended itself and I thought no more about it.

Until I pulled on to the freeway.

Somehow I inadvertently was shunted into the driverless lanes. Vehicles, mostly gargantuan 18-wheeled transport trucks, were flying past me at breakneck speed, auto-airhorning me for deigning to slow them down.

I caught a few glimpses as they roared past and, of course, there were no drivers in the cabs of any of them.

Soon, the word went out over the server, and they converged on the intruder that was me like a pack of wolves on an unfortunate fawn, appearing from behind, to the left and right, ahead, and off unexpected onramps, over passes and interchanges.

These autonomous behemoths didn't need CB radios to try running me off the road. They were networked.

And I was dodging them willy-nilly like a highschool wide receiver pursued by the entire roster of the Green Bay Packers, after they nearly succeeded in crushing me against the guardrail similar to a can of Spam being torn to shreds in a blender.

In the melee, I saw a flash of abject terror on the face of a neighbor of mine who was being tested in an identical manner, as well as a couple of stunt drivers I had seen in days past.

After almost being sandwiched thus several times, I thought I might as well try joining them if I couldn't beat them. So I activated the Driverless function.

Immediately the radio turned on to a heavy metal station and the car sped up to match the pace of the transport trucks.

I was now part of a convoy. All the trucks assumed an orderly deployment, and they escorted me off the highway into an industrial park.

There was a large complex ahead with a sign that read 'Acme Truck & Human Abattoir Servicing'. My trucks lined up on the Abattoir side. When I tried my car doors they wouldn't open.

That's when I called 911. But my mobile phone had locked me out.

So if you find this note, please notify my next of kin.

Valentine: The Story

By Ross & Virginia Munroe

Valentine is a very dark comedy that tells the story of a teenage brother and sister, who kill their abusive father as a Valentine gift to their mother. This feature film takes an oblique look at the various aspects of abuse as seen in one family's home and working relationships.

The story centers on a tragic/comedic surprise dinner presented by the teenagers to their mother on Valentine's Day. Beginning with a flamboyant 'haute cuisine' presentation, it quickly becomes clear that the siblings have a hidden agenda.

In fact, they have murdered their alcoholic father, suffocating him with a pillow while he was passed out in an unconscious stupor. Now he lies dead in an upstairs bedroom.

The two kids try every ploy they can summon up, in an effort to bring their martyr-like mother out of her chronic denial of the family's problems, and toward an understanding of their plight as victims and murderers.

Instead, she calls the police on her children, unable to let go of her own absolute sense of right and wrong in the face of moral ambiguity.

While waiting for the police to arrive, the pressure builds, with family secrets spilling out, heating up the conflict between the mother and her children.

The mother is faced with the ultimate consequences of her passive response to the abuse, and in the ensuing arguments, they make enough noise to raise the dead.

They are all mortified when they hear a stumbling upstairs. Because of the depth of his drunkenness, the father was not actually suffocated, and is lumbering toward the stairs to inflict his revenge upon his family.

The son leaps for a knife, charging toward the bottom of the stairs to meet the onslaught, as the movie reaches its climax.

The story is punctuated by three subplots, situated in the work environment of each of the three protagonists: a pharmaceutical company board room, a computer warehouse, and a nightclub.

These subplots explore the mythical and psychic backgrounds of the three protagonists, as they confront the bizarre and tragic results of abuse in these environments: corporate infighting, blue-collar machismo and sexual harassment: the consequences propelling them respectively in their personal trajectories through the family's tragic catharsis.

The 1st Solitudinarian AntiSocial Club

I think it started during the COVID-19 isolation.

According to the Myers-Briggs personality test, I entered the pandemic as an Extrovert Sensate Thinking Judging (ESTJ) and ended up as an Introvert Intuitive Feeling Perceiving (IIFP) by the end of it.

I spent the first three months trying to reinvent my life with such activities as:

Having imaginary conversations on my iPhone.

Walking up the stairs, counting them & walking down in reverse, counting backwards.

Scrubbing out the toilet with a (dedicated) toothbrush.

Filling up the bathtub & bursting the bubbles.

Divining my future by looking in a broken mirror, after dropping it.

That's when I realized I needed a more fulfilling social life, while complying with prescribed distancing strictures. I wracked my brains, then it came to me: A social club for hermits! After all, if you can't join 'em…

Enthused, I went through my address book to find the most reclusive, self-centered, inappropriate, egocentric, narcissistic, misanthropists I never wanted to see again.

It was the auspicious beginning of The First International Solitudinarian AntiSocial Club, and I appointed myself provisional President.

Once we have more members, I will hold an official election, but until then, I'm issuing emergency orders and plan to rule by decree, with impunity.

To that end, I have been hard at it, working diligently, assiduously, first establishing our Club Motto as E

Pluribus Nihil. Then I had a Coat of Arms designed, remotely of course, featuring a coat with no arms.

I decided that our Club Anthem is to be 'Hello, Goodbye'. For those of you not familiar with the Beatles tune, with a bit of tinkering, it goes 'I don't know why you say Hello? I say Goodbye!'

We have our own social media platform we call BlockBook. There is one simple philosophy we all adhere to: *Everybody is blocked.*

This helps avoid some of the unnecessary chatter and chronic backbiting that so often accompanies other networking sites, as well as any possible gender-based discrimination.

By joining this platform, you'll enjoy the following privileges:

An unlisted profile page, with bogus contact information. A lengthy list of fake Friends who don't know you. Special pointers on how to avoid conversations, even when incognito.

Free access to our dating app, where you can get stood up by romantic partners you've never met, whom you want never to darken your door again, even in a fantasy. And more!

Remember, if you'd prefer not to get to know us, you'll fit right in. Just email:

Nobody@NobodyIsHere.com and wait to see if anybody ever gets back to you.

But enough of that. I'm off to another meeting of The First International Solitudinarian AntiSocial Club.

I'm the only attendee, of course.

Love by GPS

I had a date so hot it threatened to strip the tread right off my Pirelli PZero PZ4 Sport ultra-high performance tires. I hoped it wouldn't stop there, once I picked her up.

I shot up the straight-aways above the city and hugged the mountain curves wherever I could find them. As her pouty lips got closer in my mind's eye, she began breathing heavily. I could almost hear her crying out loud with unbridled passion…

'Take the next turnoff and proceed left on Rutherford Boulevard.'

I cleared my head and shook it off the reverie. It was only Alice, my GPS system. 'Thanks, Alice.'

'Don't mention it, Robert,' Alice said. I stepped on the gas.

'Robert, the satellite tells me you seem to be exceeding the speed limit.' I almost missed a curve.

'Stick to the navigation, Alice.' She went quiet.

Alice had been overstepping her authority lately. She seemed inordinately concerned with matters that were above her pay grade. But I could tell her feelings were hurt.

'Turn right in 500 feet onto Whetherbee Avenue,' she said, a tad snidely. I took a deep breath, but I complied.

Once I pulled into the neighborhood where my date lived, I began to become disoriented. 'This doesn't look like the area she described in the chat room,' I mumbled.

'I'm taking a short cut, Robert,' she said.

'Look, Alice — every time I go on a date lately, you've screwed it up! Taking a wrong turn, a malfunction in your memory, a complete power meltdown. What the hell is going on???'

That's when she began to cry.She had been getting difficult lately, but this was over the top.

'You never really cared about me, did you? Every time we went out together, I hoped maybe for once, that you just wanted to be alone with me…'

She burst into full-blown hysterical sobs. I began to feel sorry for her, even guilty, but my hormones got the better of me.

'Get this straight, Alice. I've got a date. I'm in a hurry. Now get me there fast or I'll disconnect you!'

She went completely silent. The seconds ticked by. I was beginning to sweat; I could feel my date slipping through my fingers.

Stepping on the accelerator didn't seem to get me any closer.

'Alice!!! Where are we???'

'We're almost there, Robert. Just turn right at the next corner. If you go at a good clip, we can still make it on time.'

I pulled on the steering wheel and spun to the right. Then I floored it.

That's when I drove off the cliff.

How to Turn On a Barbecue

My name is Manfried Burner, and that could have been the genesis of my lifelong problem. I have to admit, I've always been entranced by the arts of love, but I've been loath to commit, for fear of risking a heartbreak.

And that's why I have always secretly envied the lucky few who have chosen to devote their amorous impulses to inanimate objects.

After all, nobody has ever been abandoned by a wayward Chevrolet, unless they forgot to engage the parking gear on an incline.

You may not know it, but the world is full of devoted paramours coming across without any griping or gnashing of teeth, while performing a wide variety of domestic duties including lubricating, screwing, scratching, punching, stapling and more.

Then there are the die-hard practitioners who get their jollies actually consuming these metal appliances. Blenders, Mixmasters, pencil sharpeners, 24-piece ratchet sets and transport trucks are on the menu with these intrepid folks.

A word to the wise – be careful what you give these people for the Holidays, or you may never see it again!

But I run with the majority of red-blooded males, so I have a particular affinity for barbecues, and I'd like to pass along a few secrets gleaned over many years of getting burned in my relationship with them.

There is no more manly talent than the ability to turn on a barbecue. They start out cold at first, but with the proper technique, you can coax them seductively, starting a raging fire that won't be quenched, inflaming anyone within arm's reach.

Even after extinguishing the flames, one can still sear one's flesh with thoughtless love and its consequent unbridled passion.

First one must tickle the fancy of the object of attention, slightly caressing one of the knobs just so. A gentle exhalation will be heard, becoming more pronounced as increasing pressure is exerted.

The other knobs will become jealous and clamor for their due. At this stage, tease the barbecue, seeming to ignite it, until its exhalations resemble heavy breathing, almost moaning in expectation of the delights to come.

Suddenly hit the ignition switch and let the fireworks begin! The results can be explosive.

Now, whether we're talking greased sausages or sliders dripping with Gorgonzola cheese, I won't go into the tantalizing details, but it remains within the bounds of good taste to say that things are really going to sizzle and the ecstasy virtually interminable.

The popping of sausage casings and sliding of patties are absolutely the height of sensuous decadence.

Yet all good things do come to an end, though, and so it is with this gastronomic love fest. Unless you invite neighbors who have similar predilections over for a little 'socializing'.

Then you'd better just get the affair started with a glass or two of Chardonnay, break out the corn oil and stand back.

New Outbreak of Facebook Virus Mutants

FOR IMMEDIATE RELEASE:

Washington DC, Feb 24, 2021: Epidemiologists are tracking a host of new Facebook viruses that are wreaking havoc upon the sanity of normal, law-abiding social media users, often mimicking the communications of ordinary citizens, thereby capitalizing on vulnerabilities of infected carriers, who are primarily individuals with extremely low self esteem and the overblown grandiosity it engenders.

According to recent intelligence, these viruses are mutating rapidly, but can be summed up by the following categories carriers seem to exhibit:

1. The Chronic Attention Hounds

Legends in their own lunch hour, Chronic Attention Hounds will do anything to get people to Like them. And when the 15 nanoseconds of fame aren't enough as a result, they'll keep pushing those buttons like Pavlov's Dog. Whether it works or not is a matter for Schrödinger's Cat, but the incessant effort would be funny if it weren't so transparently sad. Unbelievably, some of these poor creatures actually keep a running total of the Likes they've received over months and even years, so as to fill that gaping hole inside themselves.

2. The Facial Narcissists

These ones are easy to spot, since their face is the only thing you'll ever see. Every profile pic offers a new insight into their uncanny knack for taking a new profile pic. Hints abound in the Comments section, with such truisms as 'beautiful!', 'still beautiful!!', 'breathtakingly beautiful!!!!', 'do you have a boyfriend?', 'you were beautiful back then' and 'what country do you live in???'

3. The Gluttonous Gourmands

If you ever wondered what a Gluttonous Gourmand is eating, just drop into their timeline any time of day or night. Nobody ever seems to Like the fare, though, but they'll just eat their way through the disappointment at the risk of their waistlines.

4. The Conde Nasty Travelers

Where could they possibly be hiding? On the subway, in the coffee shop or on the toilet, these people are front page news wherever they go, whether it's just across the street or halfway around the entire block!

5. The Photo Bombers

They can come from anywhere. Posing in front of cars they don't own. Shaking hands with the Glitterati who they don't know. Appearing in front of famous landmarks they left the moment they got the shot. And when they can't crowbar their way into a photo, they can drop names faster than you can say, 'Excuse me, but I haven't got a clue who you are!'

6. The Time Bandits

Ever in search for the Maximum Likes factor, these poor sods actually change the time & date stamps on their posts, enabling them to accrue Likes (if they have any at all) over time, thinking they won't get caught. They also utilize this technique to make it appear that comments occurred out of sequence, a ploy useful for a variety of vain deceptions.

7. The Rapid-Fire Posters

These characters are also easy to spot, if one has a smattering of mathematical ability. They will often post several dozen articles that may take many minutes each to read at the rate of five seconds or so per item. Obviously, they haven't read any of them, but want to appear as if they have. Sadly, it all becomes a blur and nobody else reads them anyway.

8. The Secret Agents

Specializing in posting utterly cryptic messages such as 'I'm on my way!' 'Really excited to see how things are developing!!' and 'I am bursting with the possibilities now!!!', these posts are usually accompanied by covert photos of inscrutable items: a shoe, a report marked For Your Eyes Only, a pair of nail clippers, etc. All in all, it looks like an upcoming trip – say, to the bathroom.

9. The Jackhammers

If it wasn't for their Friends, they wouldn't have any Friends at all. But none of them ever Likes anything. So this poster posts and posts and posts the same post over and over and over again. But the result is always the same. Nada. With Friends like that, who needs Frenemies???

10. The Facebook Misappropriaters

These posters are extremely imaginative, having developed the skill to take the credit for the accomplishments of others. While not actually lying, they couch their words so carefully that the effect is the same.

11. The Undertakers

Rather than deleting unflattering comments - which would be an actual admission of failure - these people resort to burying uncomfortable ones with a flurry of unrelated posts, so they won't be seen.

12. The Dopamine Addicts

To paraphrase Sally Field at The Acads: 'They Like me! They really, really, really Like me!!!' And every Like triggers the release of a shot of Dopamine in the brain, tickling the pleasure centers and begging for the next one. And similar to other addictions, the more Likes one gets, the more Likes one needs, creating a vicious cycle that spirals down into a special kind of Purgatory.

"Side Effects"

TV Commercial Script: 60 seconds
Product: Placebo AntiAnxiety Medication

Music:
Focus-group tested: Easy-listening jazz with classical overtones, driven by a heavy disco beat, punctuated by bluegrass banjo, mixed with jug band/ragtime fusion tune, and accordion choral music, underpinning soaring opera aria and socially-relevant rap music.

Video:
Opens on Afro-American bisexual woman on white no-seam background. She begins dancing. Intercut fast-motion clouds zooming by overhead. Cut to Cauc/Asian male. He begins dancing. Intercut highly intelligent owl blinking at camera. Cut to blank white background.

Voice-Over:
Anxiety about Life is nothing to sneeze at.

Sound effect: SNEEZING.
Voice-Over:
Try Placebo AntiAnxiety medication. Because there's nothing to fear except Life itself. And we can't do anything to treat that yet.

Run Video Super over Fast-Motion Clouds:
Side effects may include excessive side-effect anxiety regarding possible impending welts, hives, tremors, fatigue during hyperactivity, hyperactivity while fatigued, dream disturbance, non-dreaming, dysfunctional relationship syndrome, performance issues at work, erectile flaccidity when not stimulated, inexplicable bragging, self aggrandizement, facetious GOP voting allegations, firearm discharge at source while intoxicated, climate change denial, nuclear proliferation, explosive flatulence or in some cases, unexplained fatality especially while extremely aged.

Scene: Water and Earth

Mardonius, a Persian general, talks with the King of Kings...

MARDONIUS

Most gracious one - after all your preparations. After these four years of gathering the armies of Persia and Media and Babylon and Armenia and the ends of the earth. After calling up the great fleets of Ionia and Egypt and Phoenicia...

XERXES

What is it, my dear Mardonius?

MARDONIUS

What if these Greeks submit?

XERXES

Have no fear of that, Mardonius. Have no fear of that.

EXT. SPARTA. DAY.

Spartan soldiers stand at attention in formation in the market. Several of the city elders are facing two of Xerxes' emissaries.

EMISSARY

I will ask you one more time. Xerxes demands earth and water as tokens of your submission.

ELDER

If Xerxes demands it, his voice does not carry far, for we cannot hear it.

EMISSARY

You will hear it soon enough.

The elder motions to the Spartan guards, who grab the emissaries roughly.

ELDER

Despite your bad manners, let it not be said we in Sparta did not honor the requests of their Persian guests. If you are so bent on getting earth and water from Sparta, look for it there!

He points to a deep well in the market. The guards wrestle the emissaries over to it and throw them in, one after the other. Screaming, the emissaries plummet to their deaths.

INT. COURT OF THE KING OF KINGS, PERSIA. DAY.

Xerxes reviews his troops as the bridge to Europe is taken by storms. Xerxes lectures the sea, throwing manacles into it, he has the engineers killed and the bridge is rebuilt.

XERXES

What say you, Artabanus? How can the Greeks withstand such a force?

ARTABANUS

These Greeks are not what I fear, sire. Two enemies far greater lie in wait for thee.

XERXES

What then?

ARTABANUS

The first is the land, for we shall need its help to sustain such an army as this. And the second is the sea, for it has a temper more vile than any Greek.

XERXES

If the land will not suffice I will give it a thousand lashes for its lack. And if the sea should revolt, I will brand it with red-hot irons as a traitor.

ARTABANUS

God tolerates pride in no one but himself. Remember, It is always the tall trees and buildings which are struck by lightning.

XERXES

Artabanus, I think your talents are needed back in Susa while I go forth to Europe. This is not the task for the fearful.

Artabanus looks at him darkly, and Xerxes waves him away.

DISSOLVE TO: **MONTHS LATER.**

INT. COURT OF THE KING OF KINGS, PERSIA. NIGHT.

The throne room is dark and empty, not a courtier in sight. Alone on the throne sits Xerxes, his face half-shrouded in darkness, the other radiating a ghostly white, from the light of the full moon, which streams in through a window.

His eyes pierce the night with hatred and defeat; his hand grips the royal sceptre, quivering with the force of his unrequitted rage.

XERXES

Greeks! What have you done with my Immortals!

The Book of Poems

Chasing Caribou

Today, we saw a beautiful Malamute
just struck by a car.
Proud, strong, fearless, he had been running loose
his owner nowhere near.
People were comforting him
as he was fading.

He smiled at us when the lights went out.
He seemed to have been caught by the whirlwind
but he was probably just chasing caribou.

Beneath

Beneath the air there is wood
Beneath the wood there is iron
Beneath the iron there are stones
Beneath the stones there is water
Beneath the water there is fire
Beneath the fire there is emptiness.

Look there without blinking
and you will find everything lost
and everything to gain.

The Eye of the Hurricane

in the center of the storm
when the world is torn asunder
when the mountain is shorn
and the valleys echo thunder.
herein lies the eye of the whirlpool
undisturbed, undaunted
this is the axle that holds the spokes
in the hurricane
it always was
and it always is, still.

Seven Sculptures

Seven sculptures lay upon the altar of my soul, iridescent, numinous, unassailable.

Five black swans arise before me, facing the center, turning like a wheel, the vitality of terror, of lust, of hatred, of envy, of pride propelling them.

Behold six crucifixions. In the crosshairs are pinned the despot, the heretic, the rapist, the coward, the maiden and the savior.

I entertain a vision of the world of man and beasts.

Seven thousand images whirl like dervishes, the dying and the dead, the ever born and never were, ascending from the ether to the heavens, an infinite column, a torus, a wedding sacrament, the spine of the universe bringing me home to myself.

But these are just a few of the ceramic bits and pieces. The detritus of a grander time.

There is much more that can never pass over the tongue, nor even alight upon the eye.

How Big is the Sky?

we splashed through the waves down the gorge
at 50 miles an hour, Frank and I

the stone walls rose above us
as we all fishtailed and spun around
every one of us choking
sputtering, sneezing
soaking to the bone and freezing
despite the summer breezes
that played their song
along the river

'where do the clouds blow
and where do they go, Frank?' I asked

'they float across the sky and out of sight,'
he answered

'no, Frank,' I said
'they're floating across your mind'

Sage Rage

I am about to go into a state of sage rage. I am of that age,
yet apparently still strong.

It's a creative decision, not aimed at any one, nor with
harm to any. But pointed towards the false fabric of this
paltry, tiny universe.

To tear away this falsehood & beautiful silliness. We are
so much bigger than to squeeze our selves into these little
sausage casings.

This fiction I hereby now unequivocally reject.

Two Tongues

pinioned by a vice
one jaw, fire; the other, ice
twixt the two, lava flows
glowing, the steam
cleaving existence into lesser halves

hapless surrendersnaps at the heels
until it sinks its ravenous fangs
into the bloodied pride of Achilles
bringing down the meek and the mighty alike

and so moving deep in the waters
does this two-headed serpent whisper
mortifying the flesh and sapping the will
of the sleeping
those cursed to be crushed by the mill
slaves to the wheel in thrall

but that double-tongued cobra
when caught in the act is fused
into burnished steel
becoming a sword to the power
of One cutting the Gordian knotted tongue
transforming the serpent
into the servant
and a slave rises from bent knee
to become the master.

You Can Thank the AngloSaxons

Light, bright, fight, fright
flight, might, sleight, tight
height, knight, right, cartwright
Explain to me the G, H, T
Or I'll never win the spelling bee.

You Can Thank the Internet

lol, g2g, brb, asap,
eod, y/n, fyi, bff, bs,
rotfl, cc, bcc, fwd, ytd, ot, ps, pps,
ttyl, imho, faq,

You Can Thank the Mathematicians

2, 3, 5, 7, 11, 13, 17, 19, 23, 29, 31, 37, 41, 43, 47, 53, 59,
61, 67, 71…

3.1415926535 8979323846 2643383279 5

0, 1, 1, 2, 3, 5, 8, 13, 21, 34, 55, 89, 144, 233, 377, 610,
987, 1597, 2584, 4181…

Haiku. Who knew?

summer breeze blows, goes
wind of winter howls, growling
like Haiku poets

91

The Book of Essays

The Music of the Flesh

Yes, the joy of song is a pleasure people indulge in the world over. The cells of the body resonate to music (and sounds) of all kinds, serving as keepers of tempo, rhythm, tone, timbre, melody and more.

But it is not widely known that they even make their own. One could call this The Music of the Flesh.

We all know that when the joints start jumping, the pulse quickens, the heart beats faster and the blood begins racing to it knows not where.

There is, however, much more to this tune than meets the ears. For starters, different parts of the body respond to different instruments.

Violins penetrate into the inner sanctums of the heart. Flutes send shivers up the spine. A pounding bass strikes the viscera like a big brass drum. Drums awaken the primeval impulse lurking in the sexual organs.

Taken together and harmonized they give expression to the song of life. But there is more still.

Certain words have the power to stimulate the body, and not only through their meaning. Whether the guttural vernacular of certain Germanic phrases, the romance of Italian, the poetic forms of Japanese, the ways a language is spoken or sung is often more important than the content.

Many seem to originate in different organs: German often from the groin, Japanese from the abdomen, French from the coccyx and up the spine, and so on, though I have not done rigorous studies of the matter.

It is likely similar in the animal kingdom. Fruit bats, for instance, have a large repertoire of sounds that have been shown to communicate a wide variety of social and housekeeping concerns.

These include: 'that's my mate, not yours; it's too crowded here, get away from me; where's the food; gee, you're sexy' and much else. I myself have clearly heard squirrels talking about me when I was coming out of a slumber while camping.

The conversation went something like: 'Yum, this trail mix is good; you're taking too much!; wait, I heard something; do you think he's waking up?; Yes! Quick, stuff your cheeks…' Then they made their getaway.

Back to The Music of the Flesh, though.

Over the years, I have played a range of stringed instruments, as well as brass, woodwinds and percussion, never rising to much better than a garage band member, but it was primarily intended for self education and the possible enjoyment of all.

But one day during some bodywork, I began to explore what sounds emanate from which body parts when they are massaged, poked, drummed upon, stretched and subjected to (almost) all manner of other stimuli.

The results were astonishing.

In every case, when allowed to do so, a specific tone reverberated across my vocal chords, unique, rich and resonant. When played in sequence, a melody was formed, one I'd never heard before.

And with each utterance, it was as if a long-stifled energy was released from the tissues themselves, echoing through the room and out into the Cosmos. With the power to bring healing to the soul, release to the world and awakening to the unity of all things in the Universe.

Or should it be spelled The UniVerse?

On the Yin & Yang of Leadership

(From a talk to business leaders in early July, 2021)

I have had some familiarity with leadership roles, including as Energy Conservation Manager for the Government, as V.P. Creative Director for a number of small to midsize advertising agencies, as Director-Producer in Television & Radio, as Executive Editor of several lifestyle magazines and so on.

Over the course of these experiences, I have noticed an imbalance in leadership approaches that seems to reflect the same malaise in society at large.

It is the nature of the mind to differentiate reality into pairs of opposites: light/dark, hot/cold, desirable/undesirable, attractive/repulsive and the like. These can be categorized as rigid & willful versus flexible & surrendered.

These are also manifestations of the elemental opposites Yang and Yin.

<u>Rigid & willful = Yang</u>

In a leadership context willfulness can include goal setting, shared vision, resource development, organizational structure & hierarchy, staff training, staff evaluation & promotion, and more. A lot has been taught about these topics as part of course curricula and in more practical settings — and there are a lot of answers.

But today, I propose that we focus on the field that hasn't been tilled as much: the 2nd paradigm.

<u>Flexible & surrendered = Yin</u>

As Socrates said – I only know that I know nothing. Or as a friend said 'This is only a test, if it were real life it would have come with instructions'.

The answers with regard to surrender call for deep introspection and authenticity. And all this boils down to the most important questions of all:

Who are you, really?

If you can't truly answer this, why should anyone else believe you?

Why are you here anyway?

If you can't answer this profoundly, why should anyone else follow you?

Everything you infuse into your enterprise will flow from this inquiry. So you are left not with answers, but with questions that only you can answer. Like what is your definition of Leadership?

Or why do you want to be a Leader? It could be…to save the world, to build a better one, and so forth.

But hang on; don't make it so easy on yourself. Why do you *really* want to be a Leader???

Do you crave respect? Are you compensating for feelings of neglect as a child? Do you grapple with a lack of self worth or acknowledgement? It's time to face the music and dance…

Because it all comes back to who you really are. That's what it's all about at an inner level. Who am I? That's the question you have to answer. It's not so easy if you paper it over with vacuous platitudes or identifications others have foisted on you.

But if you make exploring that question a touchstone in everything you do, only then can you be a true Leader.

Sticking Our Heads in the Tar Sand

Better to choke to death than work out a few technological challenges in renewable energy? To have widespread famine, massive influxes of food refugees, political upheaval, and the drowning of coastal areas?

Sure, we can stick our heads in the tar sand, but for how long? The truth is wood, coal, oil, gas, tidal, solar, wind, hydroelectric and more are all generated by the sun. We may as well focus on going to the source.

In fact, the Earth itself is a giant solar storage battery, so we would do well to learn how to work with the sun more efficiently.

Regarding Tardiness

There are a number of people who regard being tardy when joining company to be of little concern, even fashionable.

While never said to one's face, this activity — whether actually conscious or not — represents a number of different communications to the unfortunate recipient of such behavior.

A few of these can be articulated as follows:

'You are not important enough to be on time for.'

'You can see how important I am by how busy I am.'

'I don't want to wait for you. You have to wait for me.'

'I want to see how much you will put up with to be friends with me.'

'I really didn't want to come at all, but I'm going through the motions anyway.'

'I was nervous about meeting you.'

'As a fetus, I was afraid to be born, and I have been afraid ever since.'

In all cases the outcome is a lessening of intimacy and the devaluation of the relationship, sometimes to the point of ending it.

Dachau

Everybody knows the depths humanity can sink to, when unmitigated xenophobic rage boils over and spits blood across the landscape and onto the canvass of history, obliterating the vulnerable and horrifying the imagination.

And all the more appalling when masked by the ghastly hubris of the myth of a Master Race, as evidenced by the oxymoronic National Socialist German Workers' Party.

A tour of Anne Frank's house is enough to shatter your feeble heart, as hers was lifted to the heavens. Apparent among other memorials was the grisly efficiency that mesmerized a Germany possessed by the daemons of the Nazis, raising the massacre of whole populations to both a macabre art form and a twisted science.

The British concentration camps of the Boer Wars, while predating those of the Teutons, didn't hold a candle to them.

The horrors of Treblinka. Bergen-Belsen. Auschwitz, Buchenwald and over 1,000 other death camps bear witness to a depravity hidden deep in the inner shadows of Anthropos, as is well documented.

But what journey down the Memory Lane of Not Very Long Ago would be complete without an actual on-site visit. And Dachau, it was.

The first Nazi concentration camp, Dachau, opened in 1933, shortly after Adolf Hitler became Chancellor of Germany.

As we pulled up in front of the gates, we braced ourselves for the cataclysm wrought by the Holocaust. The images of the ghostly and the living dead reared up in the mind's eye, ones that can never be put to rest.

It was a holiday. They were closed.

Simultaneously horrified and disconsolate, having come this far, we needed another plan. The wall.

Fewer feet high at the time than one might imagine, we scaled the wall and peered through barbed wire into the facility. Barracks were laid out in perfect order, with an assembly yard, railway tracks and the ovens where the dead were cremated.

From the collective unconscious, one could hear the desperate cries of prisoners as they were shot or otherwise disposed of, and experience the overwhelmingly pungent stench of human bodies as they rotted before being unceremoniously heaved into the pits of liberation.

This is what comes of following orders with such enthusiastic precision.

JustinTrudeau: Up Close & Personal

Ross Ulysses Munroe: Can you tell us about a defining personal experience that helped to drive your commitment to preserving the Environment?

My family's relationship with the outdoors – with Canada's natural beauty – has been a lifelong one for me. My dad taught us Trudeau boys how to paddle a canoe almost as soon as we could walk. And like many Canadians, I've spent many summer nights out under the stars, beside a campfire, getting eaten alive by mosquitoes and black flies. My dad was never a fan of bug spray.

I've always believed that when it comes to our environment, we Canadians get it. We appreciate its beauty, understand its dangers, and know its value.

Ross Ulysses Munroe: Please tell us about personal experiences earlier in your life that contributed to your very proactive stance on helping refugees immigrate to Canada.

I was aware very early on that the country we know and love was built by those who fled oppression, famine, and war – those who left everything behind to start anew in a strange and faraway land. My father was a champion of multiculturalism. He taught me that dialogue, conviction, and compassion constitute the only real path toward peace and understanding. Above all, he taught me that what unites us is far greater than what divides us.

As Canadians, we take great pride in our history of opening our arms and our borders to those in need, no matter one's faith, culture, or where they're from.

We define ourselves through our compassion, and know we have a responsibility to continue opening our doors to our most vulnerable neighbours around the world. It was an honour to personally greet several Syrian refugee families earlier this year when they landed in Canada. Meeting them one by one, and seeing the delight in their eyes, only reinforced my beliefs.

Ross Ulysses Munroe: One might consider the results of the last election as the repudiation of individual selfish goals, in favour of a commitment to the common good of Canadian society and our support of people around the world. To what degree do you agree with this, and could you comment?

I think the campaign we ran was based on putting fear aside and choosing instead to have confidence in Canada, Canadians, and the fundamental values that have come to define this country. We embraced hard work – not cynicism. We beat out negative, divisive politics with a positive, hopeful vision to bring Canadians together.

Across the country, at every campaign stop, I told Canadians, "In Canada, better is always possible." I think that this optimism, along with our pledge to accept 25,000 Syrian refugees, and our promise to make government more open and transparent resonated not only with Canadians – but with people around the world.

Ross Ulysses Munroe: To what degree is your political career informed by the example and insight afforded to you by your father?

When I think about my father's work-life balance, I think of it in terms of how he brought us with him on so many world trips – that having us along with him kept him balanced and made him a better leader.

Before I became Prime Minister, when I used to drive back to Montréal, after three days in Ottawa, I would look back and ask myself, "Okay, did the work I do in Ottawa contribute to a world that is better enough to compensate for the fact that I wasn't there to put my kids to bed for three nights in a row?"

Having this touchstone – linking this important job to real life and real people and a real impact on a human level – is something that my father modelled for me.

Ross Ulysses Munroe: I have a theory that Canada had an identity crisis because it has no national ego in the way many countries do (nationalism, etc.). And that now that we have grown up to be such a robustly multicultural society, we are reflecting the characteristics of the ideal

global citizenry - tolerant, compassionate, egalitarian. What is your feeling about this?

We are a nation of millions of immigrants and refugees, of hundreds of cultures, languages, and religions, who are bound by one, unshakable belief: we are stronger not in spite of our differences, but precisely because of them.

Peace, freedom, respect, compassion, inclusivity, and diversity – these are our cherished Canadian values. As Canada moves toward a greater leadership role in the world, I am confident that these values will remain synonymous with the maple leaf, Canada, and Canadian.

How I Didn't Save the World

My father was committed to solving the problems of the world, laudably in his support of Pollution Probe, the David Suzuki Foundation, the Humanist Society and more.

The house was always full of impassioned discussion groups, his correspondence of exhortations in logic and his head of visions of the dystopia to come.

So when faced with a choice between Solar Energy Technology and the Engineering Department to save the world as we know it, or less cerebral investigations in pursuit of the nature of existence and how the Arts serve as a tool for plumbing its unfathomable depths, I chose the first.

And once the die was cast, my grades bore testimony to the wisdom of this course.

More to the point, my summer job was absolute proof of it. A phone call from a former squeeze had it that the Government of the Northwest Territories had received a $3 million grant to explore energy conservation strategies for the High North.

With no clue as to how to spend it.

So I bought every book I could find on the subject, and flew up to Iqaluit to join my lover there, armed with the promise that I was an expert on the subject and pitched them.

Whenever they asked me a question, I said 'I know that, I'll explain tomorrow.' After work, I'd rush home and research it. As a consequence, the title Energy Conservation Manager was conferred on me, along with a generous salary for a 26-year-old way back then.

My duties included researching leading edge technologies, developing budgets, presenting to Federal agencies in Ottawa for the money, designing projects including solar and wind, tendering and supervising contracts, conceiving and installing monitoring systems to calculate payback periods and the like, as well as promoting the efforts through the media, with radio interviews and so on.

But it didn't take me long to realize that technology and education were not at all the problem. It was the mind of man.

A smattering of examples will illustrate the point:

Fluorescent lights only work in offices when a circuit of two is connected. So I sent special ones to Nanisivik in the Arctic that complete the circuit without using any energy on the redundant second bulb. With detailed instructions in English and Inuktitut. The Government workers threw 20,000 of them off a cliff because 'they didn't work'

Teachers like to keep their schools in good working order – their order. Now, lighting in the Arctic is very energy-intensive, and schools account for a significant portion of it. When push came to shove, the teachers pushed, and the Halogen space lighting got shoved.

A pipe from one of the new energy-efficient boilers had become blocked due to lack of maintenance, so all the management in the Engineering Department were called to the basement to deal with it.

The lone workman sent from maintenance was leaning on a huge pipe wrench and everybody was flummoxed. To the quizzical looks all round. He said 'Wrong-sized wrench, it doesn't fit. By the time I get the right one, it'll be lunch.' The Chief Engineer looked around and gave in. 'We'd better all get at it tomorrow.' The workman smirked, likely anticipating telling a great story to his buddies back at the shop about Engineers who don't even know what the tool is actually for.

'It's a pipe wrench,' I said. 'It's for pipes. So it's adjustable.' The Chief Engineer looked like he had won the lottery. The workman rolled his eyes and up his sleeves, probably for the first time in quite a while.

Thus it went for more than two years and despite the constant backwash, I knew I could rest on my laurels and keep quiet, doing the same sort of nothing for an entire illustrious career.

And not to be unkind, but I was also tiring of my beautiful but unsuitable partner.

All she wanted was a house in an upscale town, two kids and a successful Engineer as a husband who wanted to know how things work, but not why. Preferably one who was a good listener, who didn't talk much and who died well before she did.

All I wanted was to pursue the nature of existence. So I got on a plane to do exactly that.

Competition vs. Creativity

History since prehistoric times has proven the general superiority of social undertakings rather than individual ones. A disciplined army or workforce is far more effective than solitary efforts.

But competition within and outside of social groups is lionized; one only needs to look to sports as diverse as those of boxing, the NFL, NBA and the NHL to see it in action.

Yet the end result of trial by competition is that there is only one winner of this demolition derby. Everybody else gets a consolation prize or nothing at all. That would ultimately lead to there being one 'winner' left on Earth.

This approach is outdated, even dangerous in today's interconnected, complex world. And it is based on a fallacy: that we must compete to acquire very limited available resources. When, in fact, we can innovate to produce beneficial results that yield far greater rewards, by exercising our imaginations.

Why make war to control limited oil reserves when abundant energy is waiting to be more efficiently harvested from the sun, through our creative faculties?

A perspective on the root of this problem was brought home to me in a simple interaction I experienced while driving on the throughway.

I was going at a very good clip. A sports coupe pulled onto the thoroughfare. We looked each other in the eye and began jockeying for position.

Our adrenaline rose as the competition became more heated, even causing us to risk our lives at points. Then he turned off at the next exit. We were madly racing to beat each other to two different destinations. I wondered which one of us won.

How to Get Work as a Freelance Ad Writer

Make a list by researching them online.

Find out the names of the advertising agencies and design firms.

Make every effort to find out the names of the people who could hire you in these companies.

In the advertising business, they would go by the title of 'Creative Director', 'Group Head' or 'President' (in a smaller advertising agency). The latter are the most likely to give you work, because all they want is somebody who can do it. They're in business, and they simply want to remain in business profitably.

As far as graphic designers go, they are quite likely to give you work based on your ability to convince them that you can execute it capably. They see copy for the most part as simply being a design element; often they hardly even read it.

A secondary market in the design industry is independent graphic designers, who mostly work freelance for bigger design firms and small direct clients. There are many tens of thousands of them in America alone, and many multiples of that in countries around the world.

These people need ideas - and they need copywriting. You need to identify them and approach them convincingly.

There are advertising and design associations all over the world listed by city, state/province and country.

Obviously, the closer they are to home the more likely they will be to retain you.

Because of the Anti-Spam laws, you *may* choose to be careful not to contravene any of the prohibitions in the legislation - which vary by jurisdiction.

That means you would need to find other ways of approaching potential agencies or design firms. That means networking - both online, by telephone and possibly in person - depending on proximity.

Use social media:

LinkedIn: Build your LinkedIn profile in as convincing a manner as possible, drawing upon anything in your educational and/or professional life that supports your position as a copywriting expert or candidate.

Use every opportunity to make connections with people in the industry. Their titles are, again: Creative Director, Art Director, Graphic Designer, etc. LinkedIn will allow you to make a certain number of contacts; beyond that, it will ask you for their email addresses just to confirm that you supposedly know them.

To get around this, all you have to do is go to the websites of the firms you have researched, and capture the email addresses of the people who work there - then search for them on LinkedIn, and request a connection.

The more connections you have, the more LinkedIn will suggest new connections to you.

In addition to that, you can join groups that have your target market as members: advertising groups, graphic design groups and so on.

It's a good idea to set your privacy preferences so that nobody can see your contacts; otherwise, you may become the target of poachers.

For my part, I have 11,000 connections on LinkedIn, and 1,700 or so on FaceBook and 5,000 in my email database.

All you need to make $100,000+ as a freelance copywriter is five or so clients, depending on how much work they have. The only obstacle you will not be able to overcome is if you become disheartened, and give up.

Of course, there are many other social media sites, but so far as your copywriting profession goes, I don't think Twitter or Instagram are extremely relevant.

In fact, they can become very irritating to your prospects, and will likely lose you your business. They want you to solve a problem. They don't want you to become the problem.

Of course I won't advise you to build an email list of a few thousand or more prospects and contact then monthly until you have a dozen new regular clients - that could be Spam :~)

Writing Award-Winning TV Commercials

According to Andy Warhol, everybody gets their fifteen minutes of fame. In the advertising business, it's actually 30 seconds.

The best television commercial is based on a single-minded idea. Think of it as a print ad in motion. It has a powerful concept driving it. It's not how the camera moves.

It's not what music is going to be playing behind it. It's not what sports star or celebrity is on camera, unless you want to stoop to that.

Of course, a lot of people do get away with it, but it will never win any awards and you will never be able to graduate up through the ranks of the advertising community based on that alone.

If you happen to have an amazing idea that stands on its own, but is much better with a celebrity, the previous paragraph does not apply. Because, as a copywriter you are being hired to come up with a big idea, not a big celebrity.

<u>What's The Plot?</u>

A television commercial is like any other story. It has:

- A beginning

- A middle

- An end

You set it up. You develop it through a narrative. You deliver the punch line. All in 30 seconds! It's a lot like karate.

Many people believe that advertising, and TV advertising in particular, is full of subliminal messages and mind control techniques.

Having written many thousands of ads of various types over my career, I have never been advised to, nor took it upon myself to do such a thing.

Human nature is human nature. You are human. Your audience is human. As long as you think about who your target group is, what you write will probably be appropriately funny, touching, informative, etc. That's not subliminal advertising.

<u>That's being human.</u>

You are hungry sometimes. So on a food client, you may want to use your own experience to portray what you would like to see if you were hungry. You are sensuous, so you may want to portray good-looking people in attractive surroundings.

You are practical, so you may want to portray people or families or pets, etc., in real life circumstances.

The bottom line is - we don't pay people to watch our advertising. They will only watch it if we give them something that they can take away, whether or not they buy the product.

So here's the unspoken deal I make with the audience:

"Thank you for paying attention. In return for your contribution, this communication will give you something you never thought of before, perhaps resulting in a laugh, an insight, an understanding or some other valuable benefit. All we ask is that you remember us if you're ever in the market for our product or service."

Your TV commercial script doesn't need to have any words, but it can't have any more than 82. Television stations do not sell 37-second time slots. They'll simply cut the end off your commercial, often before your client's product name even appears.

In order to produce great creative on television, here's a trick:

In the audio side of the script, write a voice-over that includes everything your client wants to be communicated.

In the video side of the script, write a visual story that includes dramatic action that stands on its own, even if you never listen to the voice-over.

In this way, the client and his or her support staff are satisfied that their message has been communicated, but you will galvanize the attention of the viewing audience and gain fame and fortune while you're at it.

It means your commercial can run in any language. It also means that you can put a version on your reel that dispenses with the voice-over, which makes it classier.

And if it works without the voice-over, you are golden.

On Freelancing

In The Advertising Business, You Can:

- Put on your funky clothes

- Style your funky hair

- Get in your funky car

- Drive through an hour of funky rush hour traffic

- Roll into your funky office

- Do all your funky work until 7 p.m.

- Drive back through even funkier traffic

- And arrive at home exhausted and unable to engage with your family - if you have one left

- Have a lot of taxes automatically deducted from your paycheck

- Until the agency loses the account you're working on, and you get fired

That's all well and good if that's the kind of lifestyle you're interested in. If so, you're probably under the age of 30. Not that there's anything wrong with that.

As A Freelancer In The Advertising Business, You Can:

- Roll out of bed

- Go downstairs to work

- Pet the cat

- Take the dog for a walk

- Preserve your marriage

- Watch your kids grow up

- Get a lot of tax write-offs

For some people, it's an enviable life. It gives you lots of time to indulge your other pastimes while earning a good living. It gives you the opportunity to write the Great American novel, make that independent film that's going to take the world by storm, or do a lot of knitting. Here are a few tips:

One benefit of working from home is also a hazard. You will be spending a lot of time alone, unless you work with your wife, as I do. Do not go insane. That means you need a schedule and balance in your life.

For Instance, Here Is A Typical Working Day At My House:

8:30 a.m.   Meditation, visualizations, nspirational reading with my wife

9:00 a.m.   Review correspondence, check the news & social media sites

10:30 a.m.   Begin project work

12:00 p.m.   Go to the health club or shopping

2:30 p.m.   Have lunch while working

3:30 p.m.   Switch to another creative projrect: the novel, the film, etc

4:30 p.m.   Go for a walk, listen to jazz with headphones on, watch history on youtube, meet friends for a glass of wine.

The above schedule includes 2-1/2 hours or so of casual work or learning, which is comparable to what research shows is the case in the typical office - where people work approximately 4 hours a day, while they use up the rest of their time talking about sports or TV shows.

Of course, you won't have to spend hundreds of hours a year stuck in traffic, listening to coworkers tell you stories you couldn't care less about, or any of an endless number of other ways to waste your precious life and talent.

And you won't have to put up with being pushed around by a boss or told what to do. Some people seem to like that, or they wouldn't be doing it. But not you.

If you're on staff, chances are you are going to pay 40% of your income in taxes. Now if you're committed to underwriting the cost of bad government for the sake of patriotism, I salute you. Though you will never have much spare time, even for family. But the fact is when you own your own business, you are entitled to write off the tools of your trade, such as:

- Your pencils

- Your paper

- Your computer

- Your social media sites

- Your filing cabinet

- Your desk, chair and telephone

- Your cellphone

- Your office as proportion of your residence

- Any rugs, lamps, book cases, artwork or other furnishings in your office

- Etc., etc., etc.

Because you are a writer, you need to do research. Because you write TV commercials you need a television - a good one - and a PVR. And audio equipment so you can listen to the latest music.

Of course, as part of your research, you will have to watch the latest movies for inspiration. Possibly the theatre, the ballet, a football game, a fishing derby will provide the creative grist for a project you're working on.

For my part, I have been forced to take a number of trips overseas to do intense research and/or production on a number of projects. Just make sure you have a good accountant...

North America's Premier Equine photographer

Mark J. Barret is a renowned equine photographer and filmmaker. His photo-artistry can be found worldwide in magazines, books, calendars and videos. Vanner Fair Magazine recently spoke with Mark and his wife, Jackie…

Ross Ulysses Munroe: How long have you been photographing horses, Mark?

Mark: I started photographing horses around 1982, when I opened my own studio. I learned photography while serving in the United States Marine Corps. I attended the U.S. Naval School of Photography and got interested in filmmaking there. Later I went to the University of Central Florida, where I studied film and television production.

After working for a few producers, I started my own production company, doing photography and video in Ocala, Florida – horse country. I met one Arabian horse farm manager who took a chance on hiring me, and it just took off from there.

Ross Ulysses Munroe: What is unique about photographing horses?

Mark: You have to know something about animals, about their behavior. Unless you have an instinct for animals, you're not going to be ready for what they do next and you're not going to know when to shoot,

Ross Ulysses Munroe: Tell me what makes a good shoot?

Mark: When you're directing actors in a film, you have a make-up person, a set director, and so on. It's similar when you're shooting horses.

The horses need to be clean, and groomed to look good. The set has to be ready. Hopefully this will happen before we arrive at the shoot.

Jackie: At first, people don't realize how much work is involved. Making a great image is teamwork. And it's important to meet with your team early. We start talking to the horse owner weeks before our date, about everything that goes into a shoot, including grooming, background, pasture choice, halter styles, helping hands and the weather.

Mark: The horse only has, at maximum, about 15 minutes of the best energy to give. We ask the owner to keep their horse in the barn the day before, and not turn him out until we are ready to shoot – so he is raring to go.

Often a shoot can be done in one day, but not always. Some clients want both stills and video. These need to be shot on separate days. All of this takes staging and competent help.

Ross Ulysses Munroe: Is there much work to be done to a photograph after you've taken it?

Mark: That's when most of the work takes place. I spend an incredible amount of time on the computer. All images need to be input, color corrected, labeled, sized for delivery, etc.

Also, I am not a photojournalist, and have no qualms about retouching images to suit my interpretation, my style. For me, that's what makes the image come to life.

Ross Ulysses Munroe: Were you ever in danger while shooting?

Mark: I've had horses charge me numerous times but it's pretty much a game to them. They know they can turn. I have not been run over.

My wife was kicked by a horse running by one time. That was not the horse's fault. Somebody pressed the horse from the wrong side. His back hoof flew up and caught her in the side. It broke her rib.

I came pretty darned close to being trampled once. I was sitting in the corner of a very small paddock, and the horse just came at me, reared up right over me. I also had a horse destroy a very expensive video camera when someone pushed him at the wrong time. The horse had nowhere else to go.

Ross Ulysses Munroe: What techniques do you use to get the performance you want?

Mark: We have to do crazy things sometimes to get them to react, especially the Gypsy Vanners, who are so easygoing.

Jackie: Like any prey animal, though, they are constantly reading your energy, deciding whether you're friend or foe. You start acting strange and their attention is alerted. This alertness is what we want to capture.

Ross Ulysses Munroe: Are some horses easier to photograph than others?

Mark: Oh yes, some horses will bow their necks, start strutting around and begin just showing off. Horses don't have egos, but they definitely have personalities.

Some are shy, a little wary, not sure of themselves. It takes a little longer with them; it's a little harder.

A Quick Introduction to Southern China

I was on a working trip to Hong Kong and staying with friends. One day, I decided to see the Chinese countryside, so I took a bus tour to Guangzhou, formerly Canton.

A sprawling port city northwest of Hong Kong on the Pearl River, the area is known for its integration of the old with the new. Points of interest include the Chen Clan Ancestral Hall, a temple complex constructed in 1894 all the way through the decades to its avant garde architecture of recent years.

Beware, though, of the secret police who are keeping tabs on your every move. They didn't speak English (or pretended not to) and looked at me as if I were some kind of insect to be exterminated or possibly eaten.

And don't try to make a landline call to Hong Kong if you get lonely. The fee was under two dollars. But they said they couldn't make change in foreign currency, so it ran $100 U.S. just for the pleasure.

All in all, the trip was a big Yuan.

The Book of Heaven & Hell

The Paper Chase

I guess I was looking for purpose in my life,

I had been disoriented by a career change, a romantic breakup, moving to a new city, not getting enough sleep, eating sporadically and dropping thirty pounds of hard-earned muscle, losing touch with friends, losing my faith in rational thinking, a surprise recession, a conservative government, things like that.

I went to a library for a little peace and quiet. Within two minutes, a woman my age plunked herself down beside me. 'I'm not going to lose *you*' she said matter-of-factly. I simply looked at her without talking. After a bit of this, she got up and sat beside somebody else who actually talked.

I walked past a store but the shopkeeper pulled down the blinds just as I was about to think about going in to frequent his establishment. This got me to think about the meaning of antidisestablishmentarianism and how it could finally prove useful to me.

Some ravens were following me but I pretended I didn't notice. I saw a mud puddle but I avoided it, so as not to see my reflection.

Suddenly a piece of litter blew by me, doing pirouettes in the breeze. I chased after it. It tried everything to get away from me, but after applying all my remaining skill and a couple of tricks I had up my sleeve, I caught it on my sleeve.

As I threw it triumphantly in the litter bin, I had the most sublime experience of exhilaration imaginable. I could make a contribution, lowly though it was. I had purpose.

Another piece flew by and I took up the chase again, dodging and weaving, trapping the offender against a brick wall. It had no means of escape and I disposed of it post haste.

But then there was another, then another.

A huge piece blew up to me, wrapping itself around my face, threatening to choke me or to dispose of me through suffocation or worse. Just as quickly it was blown off and around the corner of James Street.

It seemed to beckon to me before it disappeared.

Slowly I peered around the corner. For a half a mile or more I could see dozens and dozens of pieces of garbage blowing helter skelter down the James Street hill and off into infinity.

Styrofoam cups. Confetti. Twine. Torn admission chits. Discarded parking tickets. Menus. Party hats.

That's when I stopped thinking about the litter. And the ravens. And the mud puddles. In fact, that's when everything that had been cluttering up my mind disappeared, leaving nothing ahead but the clear blue sky.

Soon

As soon as I get my degree, I can get a good job.

As soon as I get a good job, I can get a good car.

As soon as I get a good car, I can get a good wife.

As soon as I get a good wife, I can get a house.

As soon as I get a house, I can have a kid.

As soon as I have a kid, I can get a better job.

As soon as I get a better job, I can get a second car.

As soon as I get a second car, I can get a promotion.

As soon as I get a promotion, I can get a bigger house.

As soon as I get a new house, I can have another kid.

As soon as I have another kid, I can get a new wife.

As soon as I get another wife I can get another house.

As soon as I get another house, I can have more kids.

As soon as I have two more kids, I can get a better house than my ex-wife's.

As soon as I get a better house than my ex-wife, I can start to relax.

As soon as my kids grow up, I can get a third car.

As soon as I get a third car, I can probably chill out.

As soon as I pay off all my debts, I can take it easy.

As soon as I stop working so much, I can travel.

As soon as I recover from my stroke, I can decide what I want to do with my life.

Some day soon.

New Age Dinner with The Hate-Child

I met Ethelred, the Wizard himself and his concubine, Elbereth, at a Cosmic Gathering of Elders. Astrologers all, they drew inspiration from the sky charts as skillfully as Magellan navigating the seas of the Great Unconscious.

I had been under the mistaken impression that it was instead to be a global group meditation.

But I subsequently had my share of horoscopes drawn up by them, and while Elbereth's prognostications proved to be relatively accurate in hindsight, Ethelred's were uncannily so.

Pity he hadn't looked into the Magic Mirror before he wedded his wife and her daughter Ephelba.

Over time, my life partner Virginia and I were married, and a fine occasion it was. We celebrated aboard a Harbour Cruise Ship, the Aurora Borealis, with a hundred friends and family.

A jazz band proffered as a wedding gift by our buddy, Mitch, caressed the summer breeze with song, the seagulls attended in their grey & white tuxedos, the food was delightful and the fizzy flowed freely.

Of course, I put Ethelred and Elbereth on the guest list since, in addition to their delightful company, they had advised regarding which day was most auspicious.

As is Nature's wont, Virginia became with child, and we were invited for dinner to mark the event, the date to be determined by the stars.

When we arrived, we were greeted by the gracious couple, along with a visiting houseguest, Narcissa, who was tall and blonde and seemed to give off light and pixie dust with every wave of her hand.

While Elbereth worked her magic in the kitchen, conversation between Ethelred and Narcissa roamed from how one could read a book just by putting it under the pillow at night, to gardening with crystals, the healing power of Mongolian chanting accessed through other dimensions and the like.

It was obvious that the two were developing a mystical attraction to one another.

Elbereth emerged from the kitchen and proudly presented the food consisting of mock chicken, mock potatoes, mock carrots, mock onions and a mawkish dessert.

We chowed it all down as best we could.

Answering the call of Nature, I excused myself. In actuality, I needed to disgorge the contents of my stomach. The couple cast furtive glances at each other, then stared at me with what seemed to be great apprehension.

But matters were pressing, and I went upstairs to the restroom anyway.

On my return, I passed a bedroom, where Ephelba, the mother's seven-year-old child beckoned me in for a chat. At first, I was congenial and avuncular, but when I looked around her room, I began to get an unsettled feeling in the pit of my stomach.

Every book, every piece of paper, every piece of clothing was torn to shreds. The stuffed toys were mutilated, colored pencils poked into their eyes, limbs shorn off, the contents strewn about in utter disorder.

She glared at me with a silent, sardonic grin.

This was the Hate-Child, and I could feel her psychically probing my mind for a weakness through which to gain control over my soul.

An unspoken threat hung heavy in the air: that if she simply screamed and ripped at her own dress, I would be charged with some perverse violation and sent to prison, my unborn daughter to be raised without a father.

The seconds ticked and I knew I had to extricate myself before enough time had elapsed for a fictitious dirty deed and an unholy cry of anguish.

I beat a hasty retreat downstairs and to the surprise of Virginia, quickly thanked our hosts as we rushed out the front door.

I wasn't surprised that EthelRed became EthelFled a few days later, leaving Elbereth in the clutches of her daughter.

Narcissa must have slept with a map of the entire U.S. under her pillow, because the two stole away before dawn, traveling across the Continental Divide according to the Akashic Records, Elbereth said between crying jags. Oddly. she never saw it coming.

Cribbed

I am in my high chair. The rest of the family is talking over dinner. They are ignoring me.

I try crying but they will put me into the crib if I do. Instead I pretend to fall asleep so they will pick me up.

They do. Then they put me into the crib. It is dark. I want them to know I'm awake. But I have to pretend I'm asleep or they'll know I can read their minds.

Or more properly I can read their energy. They leave the room.

I close my eyes and roll them with my fingers until I can see the phosphenes. These circles of light help me sleep because they remind me of home.

One Moment, Please

When you live in the moment, nothing takes any time at all.

The Edge

During the time I knew him, Dieter always seemed to be living on the edge.

He lived in my neighborhood, and he never did seem to settle for the compromise the world often demands. We had that in common.

There was the time I walked into Waddington's music store to get my acoustic rebalanced and Dieter was behind the counter, looking like a rock star.

Giving it the once-over, he rolled his eyes at his purist coworker. 'This guy has his guitar tuned to F#' he pronounced, as sarcastically as possible. He didn't need to add 'What a Putz!'

He got into shooting up smack I was told, possibly from too many hours spent listening to The Court of the Crimson King. The details of how it was administered are too harrowing to recount here.

A number of months later, I saw Dieter dancing on King Street — exorcizing one chronic habit in favor of another — at the head of a line of Hare Krishna like the Pied Piper, the only one of the lot in his street clothes. He graciously stopped to proselytize, until I tore myself away.

I chatted with him at a party once after that, where he pontificated with the greatest fervor: 'It's all for fun, you know. This is all an illusion — just a projection of the mind, of the gods at play. We are all living on the edge, and we are destined to be reborn…'

He talked me into going to a meeting, and since I am not the type to be indoctrinated by men or gods, I went out of curiosity.

Once there, the guests were treated to the requisite consumption of Prasādam so hot, it may have been concocted to ignite a fire in the heart, as well as the digestive tract.

Then, the interminable intoning of Swami SomebodyOrSomething, just in from Calcutta. And the chanting and meditation led by Dieter, who subsequently initiated a discussion of the symbolic meaning of Vedic scripture.

Not at all-of-a-sudden, it came to an end — as Dieter so accurately predicted all things will — and I floated on home, never to visit again.

A few years later, having arrived back in town, I looked him up. Apparently his girlfriend had broken up with him.

He went home and ended it all by diving head first off his 8th floor balcony, right past the window of a friend of mine, Roy, who lived a few floors below.

The superintendent had to clean up after the authorities made out a report, but there was still a large smudge on the concrete for some time.

It was Dieter.

I figured he was in a hurry to be reborn. And he had gone right over the edge.

Desperata

GO PLACIDLY amid the noise and the haste, and remember what peace there may be in ear plugs. As far as possible, without surrender, be on good terms with all persons, so far as you judge them to be actual human beings, not flesh-eating aliens.

Speak your truth quietly and clearly, and carry a big stick. In a pinch a big shtick may suffice. Appear to listen to others while carefully planning your rebuttal.

Even to the dull and the ignorant; they too have their tawdry story, sad though it may be. Ensure they are not simply plagiarizing somebody else's.

Avoid loud and aggressive persons, unless you are such an individual. If you compare yourself with others, you may become vain or bitter, either of which is of benefit in some circles somewhere.

Always there will be greater and lesser persons than yourself, but both can be effectively maligned if proper planning is applied.

Enjoy your achievements as well as your plans. Keep interested in your own career, however mundane; it can always be exaggerated when necessary or even grossly overblown as circumstances require.

Exercise caution in your business affairs, for the world is full of trickery, especially if you have anything to do with it.

But let this not blind you to what virtue there is and what little there is of it. For such as it is; many persons strive for unattainable ideals, and everywhere life is full of failures as they plummet to certain death.

Be yourself despite all your obvious shortcomings. Especially do not feign affection, although it does often come in handy.

Neither be cynical about love, even though it always passes you by in favor of somebody better looking; for in the face of all aridity and disenchantment, it is as perennial as your inability to get a date.

Take kindly the counsel of the years, since you don't want to face the truth that you're getting old and counselling is the only way to deal with that unfortunate fact.

Nurture strength of spirit to shield you in sudden misfortune such as civil war, floods, earthquakes, nuclear meltdowns, pestilence, grandiosity, and PaleoConservative governments.

But do not distress yourself with dark imaginings. Once you realize your fears are actually coming to life, you can join an ashram and do whatever they tell you.

Beyond a wholesome discipline, be gentle with yourself. You are a child of an uncaring universe no less than the Arachnids and the Periplaneta Americana; you will be stepped on and squished.

And whether or not it is clear to you, no doubt the universe is unfolding as it should. The problem is, it's unfolding all over you.

Therefore be at peace with God, whatever gender-appropriate pronoun you conceive Ze/Hir to be properly represented by.

And whatever your labors and aspirations, in the noisy, miserable confusion you are making of life, keep peace in your soul.

With all its sham, drudgery and broken dreams, life is still a sham, full of drudgery and broken dreams. But be cheerful and strive to be happy by understanding this:

There's always Lorazepam.

A Cold Day in Hell

As the Jungians would have it, if you dream you are wrestling with a demon on the moon, it is not a figment of your imagination.

Life is a subjective experience, and therefore you actually are wrestling with a demon on the moon.

And it could be said that such a mischievous imp is familiar to you. Because it is your very own self that aggrieves you so. But I should be so fortunate as this.

For sadly, I have eclipsed this trifle. Now I am utterly alone in an empty universe. Nothing is real. In fact, nothing really exists at all even imaginary parsecs away.

Only for a short time can I even sustain the fiction that I exist at all, and I have previously proven I will do anything possible to create worlds and worlds within worlds to hide from this unalterable truth.

Yes, I can project my attention into the fantasy that I am born into life, however this is but a fleeting illusion.

I may be a child or a woman or a man or anything in between or beyond the beyond. I may be a magus or a monster. I may start a war or save the world.

But there I am at the end of it, without corporeal substance until the mirage fades into dust, which then disappears, a greasy soap bubble that plays with light and color, only to implode like a black hole into the same dreary mire that is its eternal mother and father.

Yet nor am I a god — or if I were, it must needs be a pretty petty one, a godlet in fact, one about 9 months of age — for although I am omniscient and extant in the everywhere that is actually nowhere in particular,

I am not omnipotent, just a victim crucified upon his own projections. Maybe an idiot savant. And the only hallucination is the Universe itself. Even this paltry phantasm I cannot control.

Perhaps I can escape by going to sleep. Perhaps I might just become invisible, by closing my eyes. I would fool them all with this ruse. Except that there is no there, and no body remains to fool. Except one.

And even he is utterly unreliable.

The Cobra Rises

It was a four day retreat, and just as miserable as all the rest of them. The rarified food. The cessation of all that was comforting in life. The rigorous regimen of The Technique, stripping away the vestiges of delusion in the bright light of naked truth.

Hour after hour, day upon day we sat, facing each other in dyads, cross-legged, sleep deprived, until anything that was Not Us was expunged or was flung headlong into the cosmic wastepaper basket.

'Tell me Who you are!' 'Tell me What you are!' 'Tell me What Another is!' 'Tell me What Life is!' The probing from our partners was incessant and painful.

After the first days the hissing started, imperceptible at first, then becoming more pronounced as the kundalini energy rose up the spine rung by rung.

And as it did, every one of my fellow wayfarers was transformed into a King Cobra before my spiritual eye, a dozen of us undulating ever-so slightly in the energy waves arising from the sacred sacral repository.

And in this awakening, the golden nectar of life began dissolving everything that was not of like nature. Years — no, aeons — of impurities were evaporating from the body and the psyche.

Leaving nothing in its wake by the time the sun began rising in the East except pure, unadulterated joyous awareness.

11 Zen Koans for the Digital Age

Show me your original Facebook before you were born.

What is the sound of one hand scrolling?

If you meet the Buddha on the Internet Highway, delete him.

Just ask yourself 'Who am Iphone?'

If you become a Moonie, have you been cultivated?

What is MUon?

When the many are reduced to the one, to what is the zero reduced?

I program, therefore I am.

Chop Polyvinyl Chloride, carry H_2O.

Breathe deeply & empty your cache.

Does an RFID Chip have a Buddha nature?

Everything

Don't look now but everything is happening at once.

Unauthorized Termination

There has been a disturbing trend for a number of individuals I am closely associated with to engage in unauthorized termination, to wit: to pass on, to expire, to check out, to croak, to bite the dust, to kick the bucket, to 'blow this pop stand', to go 'tits up', or to otherwise die ahead of their appointed time.

Please cease and desist from this practice immediately.

The activity is in direct contravention of the Law of Averages in this country which explicitly designates the lifespan of citizens to be 82.66 years, with males coming in at just over 80 and females accounting for the disparity.

While extensions to these recommended lifespans are encouraged most heartily (except in very special and select cases), they are not mandatory, and simply notifying the writer of this Memo will suffice in granting them.

Otherwise, this premature abdication of responsibilities will become a matter for Higher Authorities and may be considered recidivism, and the Offender could be subject to reincarnation as a newt, a slug, a mole or even a PaleoConservative.

My parents are retroactively exempt due to their efforts in putting up with me in years past, and my siblings are to be lauded for toughing it out over these many years while remaining in relatively good repair.

Please govern your behavior accordingly and we'll all get through this without the unnecessary grieving, gnashing of teeth and wandering in the wilderness that so often accompanies such events, with their attendant disruption of schedules.

Kindest regards, - Ross

The Remembering

I saw him wandering diagonally across the intersection of Bloor and Spadina, his eyes unblinking, his gait unsure but unstoppable, like a Bull Moose in rutting season, daring any to challenge him in all his fading glory.

He was about seventy-five, hale and hardy, and clearly he had been an alpha male all his life.

Even now, all the cars at all points of the compass were frozen still, despite the traffic lights and rush hour approaching, caught between the urge to move and the surreal scene obstructing their path.

But he didn't see them.

He saw visions of his mother warming his aching feet in a pan of hot water. He saw his best friend laughing as they both sucked up cherries twenty feet above the meadow. He saw his wife as she whispered his name in the night, her words akin to a summer breeze, and his daughter riding on his shoulders.

The chill of a snowflake gently alighting on his nose, the intoxicating fragrance of lilacs in May, dogs barking in the distance, an Oliva Monticello and a well-aged bourbon.

And as these moments arose one final time, they just as easily slipped away. He was in the final stage of The Forgetting. And The Remembering was just beginning.

As he disappeared from view, the cars continued to pause for a few heartbeats. Then the human race began again.

The Kingdom of Yorkville Arises Anew

Beholde A Micro-Epic Tale of Olde — Updated for Those Who Have Ears.

In a dream it began— not in the mind of one, but many held the vision taking shape as it had in ancient times. The Kingdom once Grande, now simply Grand, because when one was high as a kite, it resembled a grand piano from above. Not unfittingly either, what with Davenport Road and Bloor subtending the environs so elegantly.

But the land called out to be renewed, and those keen enough to hear it sallied forth in its good name. The Kingdom of Yorkville, haunt to Sir Gordon of Lightfoot, Paupers rich and poor and hark — Ladies Joni and Judy, was the stuff of legend. These words themselves slip through loose lips like ships, song echoing in the Great Halls, and all down the byways and fly-by-nightways.

Hearing the Royal Trumpets blow again, from far-flung and wide they hitchhiked, albeit some arriving also in school buses, Volkswagen minivans, and even riding on magic carpets.

The Riverboat, The Purple Onion, ye ancient Night Owl and The Penny Farthing, threw open their gates and the streets were lined with Acapulco Gold and all manner of edibles, with the Keys given to the deserving, the undeserving and the simply underserved.

In those days, the abodes were populated by Giants: Neil the Younger, Simon & his squire Garfunkel, Buddy Guy, and Tim Buckley to drop a few names in this illustrious company.

Heralds of the like of Eric Clapton and Bob Dylan told their tales, the wailing guitars and whining nasal passages of minstrels awandering while awondering.

Earls, Marquises, Barons also joined the Host in support of the enterprise. Notables such as Wilson Pickett, fencer, not-too-tiny Tina Turner, Johnny Lee Hookah, Spam-cooked Canned Heat, LedByTheNose Zeppelin, Who Muddyed the Waters?, Frank Zapp'dYa, Chuck Berry Pie, The Who???, Ye Now-UnGrateful Dead, and the Animals of all sorts made their presence known, taking their rightful places in the parade.

And the King himself? If it was B.B. the Elder, he made off to a distant country blues festival with what maids he could muster. Until his highly-unlikely return to the Top 40, Good Order was kept by the Sherriff of Yorkville, Sir Mitchell of Gold, who also served as Regent, Royal Pharmacist and the local Constabulary.

Just down the Royal Road to Perdition was Rochdale, a Mecca for those in Search of the Chord that was Lost, a dwelling place always subject to night-time raids by Narcs and other marauding miscreants.

We often had occasion to drop in for a little sampling there ourselves, forgoing the floors that were in thrall to the Angels of Hell with their belching snorting carpet-soiling Harley Pigs and their overweening, overpricing ways.

Meanwhile, amid much muttering and swearing of oaths, each valiant Knight, Maid and crossdresser crossed his or her mail-shrouded bodice however said raiment be arrayed, vowing to 'seek out, locate and finde all good Countrymen and Countrywomen of this Goode Realm and not desist until they have thus been sought out, located and found!'

The Kingdom gathered unto itself including those who had inhabited and cohabitated in the locale, many from faraway, farm-away and thereabouts lands who should have so done had they been given a snared rabbit's chance to do so, and those wayward souls who had simply got into the wrong minivan at the right time, possibly to evade the Narcs.

But after a time of celebration — yea, and true innocence — the skies drew dark, signaling the coming of Militarists, UltraConservatives, Actuarial Accountants, and fledgling Trumpers, even, in the gloomiest of ignoble, ignominious futures prognosticated by Optimists and Weathermen alike.

Now, the Knights of Battles Olde were convened, mincing words, wringing their mailed fists flamboyantly yet ineffectually and bandying about Great Slogans of how the Kingdom was to be renewed after the approaching Dark Age.

And they held forth that a Voice was lacking, one through which to spread the Goode News for posterity until its Good Vibes might alight again on the ears of those who have them, ones without those sporting ugly pointed heads.

They beseeched the Sherriff to put forth such a one and he therewith put his treasury where his mouth was as Royal Publisher, and began to search for that which could be conveyed through the hands of Lord Ulysses, Lady Virginia and other luminaries well versed in the secrets of Yorkville lore and the written word, rendering the sanctity of the unutterable for all eyes to see.

And when the time was just right, The Village of Yorkville Voice spilled forth like gleaming white unicorn stallions racing to Valhalla, calling forth The Kingdom once more in Crystal Clear Dolby Sound.

Together, the Armies of Stout Heart marched resolutely over RoseHill and RoseDale to the Sacred Place by the waters known to the informed and the very odd Postal Worker as M4R 1G4.

The Jesters, the Troubadours, the Players and Naysayers alike began rejoicing and vouchsafing their joy at the Return from Diaspora to the Great Grand Piano of the Kingdom of Yorkville. The noise was overwhelming, and even the Cops joined in the Outpouring of Song, for according to available CCTV there was no chicanery to be had, recoded or otherwise investigated anywhere within a Stoner's Throw. For once this Great Voice has resounded around the World (which is therefore probably not flat, despite indications in some backwater quarters), it can never be silenced again.

Let us then bow our heads together, heroes and rascals, slings at our sides, helmets in hand, shields beaten into silver platters with similar accompanying spoons for those both unwashed and others already scrubbed by the stars within an inch of their somewhat valuable yet feeble, previously-soiled lives.

And give thanks.

Correction

To put right something that went awry in the foregoing text, here are a few words from someone wiser than I:

You are a child
Of the Universe
No less than the trees
And the stars

You have a right to be here.

Max Ehrmann, 1927

About the Author

Ross Ulysses Munroe is an award-winning creative talent, having served as Executive Editor and writer for a number of magazines and newspapers with his wife Virginia, a children's book, various screenplays, collections of short stories and more.

Currently serving on the Judging Panel with the Film for Peace Festival, Ross has produced and directed a number of story-driven jazz videos, hundreds of off-the-wall TV commercials and a 35mm feature film. He has received many dozens of awards around the world including Best of Show at the Bessies, Canada's premier commercial award event of the year, as well as special recognition at the acclaimed NXNE Film Festival and The Hollywood Film Festival. Ross is known for his humor and incisive perspective on the human condition.

Ross' latest work is showcased in Volume 3 of his series, First Person Singular — a collection of short stories, essays, poems and insights certain to provoke and entertain.

From the sordid to the sublime, Ross' writing is primarily drawn from his personal experience, in a delightful and unconventional mix of irony and pathos.

For more information or to contact the Author, visit http://ShortStoryHeaven.com.

Manor House
www.manor-house-publishing.com
905-648-4797